WHISPERS OF THE DRAGON

SARAH BRIANNE

Young Ink Press Publication
YoungInkPress.com

Edited by CD Editing
and Diamond in the Rough Editing
Cover Art by Obsidian Rose Covers

Connect with Sarah,
facebook.com/AuthorSarahBrianne
instagram.com/authorsarahbrianne
youtube.com/sarahbrianne-author
SarahBrianne.com

The flame that burns twice as bright, burns half as long.

— *LAO TZU*

I

INVISIBLE STRING

A young Ryu sat under the Sakura tree that had stood in this same spot since the dawn of time.

He looked up at the towering ancient being. The cherry blossoms stayed the perfect shade of pink, regardless of time. And, even though he was seven years of age, he had never seen so much as a single leaf fall.

"Son," his father announced his presence before taking a seat beside him, "I heard you were late to your training."

No longer looking up toward the sky, Ryu's eyes went to his fiddling feet as he grumbled, "It's not fair."

His father's voice turned stern. "You're a Tei; speak up when you have something important to say."

"It's. Not. Fair." His voice matched his father's strong tone as best as he could at his age. "It's not fair that I can't play and go to school with the other kids."

"That's because you are not like the other kids," his father, Tatsu, answered honestly. "You never will be."

Going back to kicking his feet, Ryu lifted up a patch of grass as he mumbled under his breath again, "Then why do I look like them?"

Playfully, Tatsu hit his son's shoulder with laughter. "You won't for long."

Great, he thought, knowing what was coming in a few years. "By then, everyone my age will *really* think I'm weird, and I'll *never* have any friends."

"We're meant to protect them, not befriend them, Ryu," His father told him the harsh truth of being a firstborn Tei son.

Their lineage had quickly found out it was best to keep a distance and professional demeanor with their people, all except for one.

"But, in return, you'll get something far greater than a friend."

"What's that?" Ryu finally stopped kicking the ground to look at his father.

Tatsu took a deep breath during which you could see him contemplating something on his son's features before he released it, figuring it was time to tell him. "Do you know why this tree's blossoms never fall, but all the other ones in the village do?" He looked up at its beauty like his son had just moments before he sat beside him.

"Mom told me it's a magical tree, just like you and me."

"It is." Tatsu nodded in agreement with glossy eyes shining only for a second before it passed. "And just like us, this tree is tied to you, me, every firstborn son who came before us, and every firstborn son who shall come after us ..."

Ryu's brows furrowed up at the beautiful, vast Sakura tree that sat in a secluded part of their family's property. Looking around, he finally made the connection of just how protected the sapling was when his father continued.

"Until its time and the Tei's time ... runs out."

"What?" He snapped his face to the older version of

him. Fear for his family shone in his young eyes. "What do you mean? When will tha—"

"It's all right, son." Tatsu placed a calming hand on his son's shoulder. "This tree is like a timer," he began to explain the magical powers between the living beast and them. "When a Tei son is born, the Sakura tree connects to that generation's son, setting the timer, and it isn't until his son is born does the tree make its new connection as the clock resets."

Now when Ryu's eyes met the magical tree, he could almost feel what was like a string between them. He watched the pink blossoms floating lightly in the breeze, silently wondering how he had missed it all the times he had sat under its shade, which was at least once a day.

"However"—he cleared his throat before his father's wondrous tone turned serious as he continued explaining the connection—"soon, the first cherry blossom will fall, and they'll continue to do so until *you* find your fated mate."

"My fated mate?" Ryu asked, scrunching up his face in childlike disgust.

"Your future wife," Tatsu said, laughing at his son's expression. "One day, when you're older, you won't think it so odd."

Yuck, Ryu thought doubtfully.

"And look at the bright side. You'll no longer feel lonely."

Ryu's expression slightly softened, supposing that was true. "Was Mom yours?"

Solemnly, his father nodded his head. "She was."

"Does that mean you're lonely now?" Ryu asked another question, like all children do when learning something for the first time.

"From time to time," his father admitted before bringing his son closer to him. "But you keep me plenty company these days."

Ryu chuckled, even though his heart began to feel heavy for his father. He had only felt sadness for himself for losing his mother, but now he understood the gravity of his father's own sadness.

"How did you know she was your fated mate?"

"Oh, you'll know," his father said, giving his own chuckle. "Unlike everyone else in this village, and even on this earth, you'll have the ability to know. It will be like"—a soft smile touched his lips in remembrance—"magic."

Ryu trusted he would since he now felt the magic in the tethered string between him and the massive being, but then he felt that string ever so slightly loosen what was once so taut as a single cherry blossom fell from a swaying branch.

They watched it float in the wind until it poignantly landed in Ryu's somehow knowingly waiting hand.

He gulped, beginning to understand something. "And if I don't find ..."

His father confirmed his thoughts as he trailed off, knowing it was a lot to put on his son, but it must be done all the same. "You'll need to find your fated mate before the last cherry blossom falls. If not"—he gave his own dry throat a swallow—"then you'll be the last of us to exist."

Numbly, Ryu stood, his boney knees buckling. He could barely walk as he began following the invisible string.

"Don't worry, son." His father sensed the earth-shattering weight he had just placed on the still tiny shoulders. "You'll find her, just like I did, and our hundreds of ancestors before us. A Tei always does," he assured him. It was clear he was now rethinking telling him today. "Then, when your son is born, the Sakura tree will magically rebloom overnight and stay that way until you tell him what I just told you, and what I was told at your age, too."

Closing the distance, Ryu didn't look back as his father continued to himself.

"The cycle will go on, because *it must*."

Ryu had already been told of his purpose, why he had been born and why there must be a new son born every generation. It was the same reason he was secluded from children his own age, why he was forced to train every day, and why when someone approached his father, they bowed, the same way everyone in the village would one day bow to him.

Slowly, his small hand reached out and placed his palm on the solid bark. It took only a moment before he felt it ...

The ticking.

2

YOU MUST SEEK

The Sakura tree that used to stand lush and proud now looked dull and barren with only about a quarter of its beautiful cherry blossoms left.

And that wasn't the only thing that had changed.

The connection between tree and boy had been strong, but between tree and man, it was now weak.

Where the sacred tree had become frail, Ryu had grown into a man worthy enough to carry the Tei family name. It was as if he had stolen its life force with each inch he had grown, and now that he stood at six foot six, with a strong enough build to take down any Komainu, there was not much else to take besides the remaining blossoms still holding their glory.

Nor time to spare.

"It's dying," Ryu spoke once he heard the footsteps. He'd never heard the footsteps approach behind him before, but like Ryu and the tree before him, his father had aged over time as well.

When the heavy footsteps paused beside him without a response, he looked at his father. Being able to visibly see how much time had passed on the tree, he was able to pay attention to just how much time had actually passed on his father's features. Time had at least been kinder to him than the tree, but his father's light feet weren't the only things that had changed, as silver sprinkled the sides of his once jet-black hair.

"I have looked into the eyes of every woman in this village three times over," he began, pleading for his father to hear him for what felt like the hundredth time.

"Then tomorrow, you will do it for the fourth—"

"There is no time left!" Ryu's thundering voice echoed out so strongly that three cherry blossoms fell with it. Staring down at the precious, scarce pink flowers, he took a shuddering breath. "There will be no village if our lineage dies out. Father"—he waited for him to finally look at him —"are you willing for me, *your son,* to be the last Tei in existence?"

The response he was finally given was one Ryu hadn't expected.

"It is time to see Itako."

The front door was open before they even approached, and if that wasn't telling enough that they were already expected, the old woman sitting at the tiny table in the darkened home only confirmed it.

"Ryu, I've been waiting for your visit for a long time now."

Quickly adjusting his eyes after entering, he understood why she made no qualms about getting up to greet them when he saw the all-whites of her eyes.

"Itako." He bowed respectfully before he took the waiting seat across the table from the blind lady. "Thank you for seeing me."

"I have been waiting," she repeated with disappointment while somehow looking straight at his face before her hunched-over body managed to turn to his father, who was still standing at the door. "Come in, Tatsu. I've been waiting many moons for you, too."

It wasn't a coax but a command, leaving Ryu stunned. It had been a long time since he'd heard his father addressed in that manner, and even though Tatsu didn't seem to falter as he royally entered, Ryu could sense the uncomfortable fear within as he watched his father be the one to bow to someone else for the first time.

"You've avoided coming to see me," Itako spoke with an otherworldly wisdom. "Let us see what your insolence cost us, as there is no time to waste."

Ryu's hands that he had clasped together on the table were suddenly grabbed by thin, withering ones.

"Ahh," Itako breathed, as any remaining candlelight in the home disappeared before it slowly returned. "I see now."

It was Tatsu who eagerly asked, "What is it? What do you see?"

The look on the blind lady's face told them she would roll her eyes if only she could. "It is not only a fated mate that you must seek, but a soul mate."

Ryu gave his own look, clearly confused. "Are they not one and the same?"

Itako merely laughed. "No."

"I don't understand," he said when she didn't go on.

"A fated mate are two souls destined to be together in

this lifetime," she began explaining. "A soul mate are two souls destined to be together in *every* life."

"I see." Tatsu wiped an exasperated brow that was beginning to sweat. "So, it's even harder to find."

"Eh." Itako shrugged nonchalantly. "Fated mate, one in a million. Soul mate, one in two billion."

His father had to finally take the other chair.

"Oh ..." Ryu breathed, knowing exactly what his father was feeling at this moment. "Now, I see."

"Told you." Itako palmed the back of Tatsu's head that was finally in reaching distance to her short stature. "Should have come to me sooner."

Rubbing the back of his head, Tatsu clearly thought better than hurting a hundred-year-old blind bat. "You know why I didn't want to come."

"Yes," the woman answered, all knowingly. "She told me you wouldn't."

Both Ryu's and his father's skin went pale.

"The spirits of the dead want us to honor them, Tatsu, not fear them," she said, placing a frail hand over his now. "Or have you forgotten your faith after all this time?"

With glistening eyes, he shook his head. "I have not."

"Then you must trust in Kana to protect your son, as you know his fated mate is not here."

Tatsu cleared his throat as a tear streamed upon his cheek from hearing his late wife's name for the first time in years. "I will."

"You will?" Ryu asked as shock overtook the depths of sadness from the topic of his mother.

"He must," Itako said simply, "or village life as we know it will cease to exist, along with the Tei family name."

Reluctantly nodding his head in agreement, Tatsu finally gave his blessing for his son to leave the village.

Every day, every single *day,* Ryu had questioned, doubting his mate had even been born in this village, but his father had assured him they always were. But if that was true, then: *why now?*

"It has happened once before to a Tei," Itako spoke clairvoyantly, reading his mind. "Ka Tei also had a soul mate who wasn't a child of this village, yet she somehow wandered into it."

"How?" he fervently asked, only more confused.

She gave another shrug, as if it was all so simple. "Ka Tei's mate said she could see it."

Both father and son looked at each other, knowing that wasn't supposed to be possible ... but still, hope shone in their eyes.

Tatsu let out a sigh of relief that maybe his son didn't have to leave after all. "So, she could wander in any momen—"

"No." The blind bat swatted him again. "His soul mate's different."

It looked like he was contemplating hurting an old witch this time, but then she continued.

"She's broken, 'cause he waited too long to go find her," Itako scolded him again. "Should have seen me sooner. All your fault."

His father guiltily rubbed the back of his head where he had been struck. "Oh."

Broken? Ryu suddenly grew concerned for a woman he had yet to meet.

"Yes, broken," Itako repeated clearly so he would begin to understand the girl who awaited him as she placed her thin hands over his strong ones again. "In every life, you have sat on a throne, Ryu. Together, as your two souls become whole."

Chills went up his arms, starting from where she touched. He didn't know if it was from learning he was always a king or ...

Does that mean ... I'm broken?

This time, Itako didn't answer his thought out loud, sparing him his dignity in front of his father by quietly nodding her head.

Everything Ryu thought he knew about himself changed in a single moment, knowing one thing to be true.

It was better to never be a king at all than to always be a broken one.

3
A MONSTER

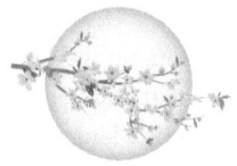

When the sun started filling up her room, she finally gave up on sleep. Most nights, she barely slept a wink, so most days, she walked around torturously tired. It was clear already that today wasn't going to go any differently than yesterday, or the day before that.

After getting dressed for the day, she walked out of her little bedroom to find her grandparents in the kitchen. Her grandfather sat at the tiny table while her grandmother shuffled around in her slippers, throwing things in the tea kettle on the stove.

"Good morning," she greeted them what seemed to be louder every day when they didn't hear her walk in. It was a blessing and a curse they had lost most of their hearing. A blessing they no longer heard her nightmares when she actually did get some sleep, and a curse they had gotten old.

"Morning, Eira," her grandmother shouted, not looking away from her concoction. "Tea is almost ready."

Eira went to the cabinet to pull out three porcelain

teacups. Placing one in front of her grandfather first, she gave him a smile, hoping he'd hear her this time. "Morning, Grandpa."

Her grandpa just smiled and gave a quick nod, showing that he still clearly didn't hear her.

She tried not to laugh at his obliviousness. These days, he wasn't a man of many words, anyway. Hell, her grandma spoke enough for them both.

One day, she hoped to be like her grandpa, just simply happy and grateful to wake up every day alive. Nothing troubled him, and everything was done for him by either his wife or Eira. It never bothered her. She loved helping her grandparents, and nothing fulfilled her grandmother more than caring for her husband.

Her grandfather had spent most of his life on a fishing boat, providing for his family, so his body had given out due to arthritis. Hence the tea her grandmother was still doting over.

"Be careful; it's hot," her grandmother made sure to always remind her husband when she was finally satisfied with the taste and began pouring the piping-hot green liquid into his cup. She then went to pour Eira some but quickly stopped when she caught her granddaughter's image. "This tea won't help you."

"It's fine," Eira said, knowing what was coming.

Her grandmother went to touch the dark hollow under her granddaughter's eyes before she quickly remembered not to make contact. "You need tea to make you sleep. Not sleeping makes you look old and ugly. Then you'll never get a husband."

"Yes, you must get a husband." Grandpa nodded in firm agreement.

"I do not *need* a husband," Eira told them for the

millionth time, not taking any offense to how they were raised to believe. "I have you both, anyway."

"We're old and ugly," her grandma stated. "You can do better. You're still young and beautiful."

Eira no longer thought of herself as beautiful, but instead of talking about herself, she laughed, taking the topic off her. "That's not true, Grandma. You're beautiful."

Her grandmother didn't yell this time, speaking in an octave only Eira could hear. "Okay, only he's gotten old and ugly."

This time, Eira had to stifle her laughter, not wanting her grandfather to ask what was so funny.

Sitting down, Grandma began filling up her own cup. "You need to go to the market and get things for your tea tonight. We're all out."

Eira didn't doubt they were, but she knew why she *really* wanted her to go to the market.

Blowing into her hot cup, her grandmother couldn't help a sly smile. "And tell Kenji I said hello."

"Yes, you must go get a husband." Grandpa nodded in firm agreement, revealing his wife's true intentions, as if they weren't obvious enough already.

Oh my.

Refraining from rolling her eyes, Eira got up, grabbed her tote, and headed for the door.

"My bones are telling me rain is coming, so don't be gone long, Eira, I want you hom—"

"Okay, okay, I got it!" she yelled back over her shoulder, in a rush to get going.

Quickly, she headed into town for the little market she frequently visited throughout the week, thanks to her grandmother. It was as if she fully expected her granddaughter to simply bring a husband home one day.

She scoffed, blowing a raspberry. *First of all …*

If Eira did want to bring home a husband—*which I don't*—it wasn't that easy. It wasn't like men just fell into your lap. *Well,* not a good one, anyway. Plus, her grandparents seemed to always forget two things.

Eira looked the way she did, and she did not like to be touched.

Hell, she didn't know much about having a husband, let alone having a boyfriend, but she was pretty sure looking and/or touching was frequently involved. Therefore, she was destined to die alone. Frankly, she had come to terms with that years ago.

While she used to dream about getting married one day, like most girls, she no longer did. These days, she only dreamed about finding peace.

When she entered the market, she kept her head down, trying to conceal her face as much as she could with her veil of hair as she went through the stands, buying the few things her grandmother needed to make her special bedtime tea.

The worst part was her hair didn't help much from people staring at her as the color wasn't common in these parts of the earth. She was just thankful not many people lived in the village, and most were used to the sight of her by now, avoiding eye contact with her as much as possible.

The last thing she needed was a root, and it had the young stand owner smiling from ear to ear when she came to buy one from him.

"Hello, Eira."

"Hi, Kenji." She tried her best to smile politely. It was easy at home with her grandparents, but out and with people she didn't know or trust, it was hard.

"More root again?" he asked, continuing to smile.

"Yes, please."

When he handed her the wrapped-up root, she knew Kenji was on her grandmother's side, as he always seemed to give her the smallest bundle so she'd have to come back.

Placing it in her tote with the other things she had accumulated, she pulled out the money and set it on the counter stand, not into his waiting hand. "Grandmother wanted me to tell you *hello*."

"In that case, it's free." He slid the money back closer to her. "Tell her I hope to see her next time."

"I will." Eira forced another small smile, knowing it was pointless to argue with him to keep the money since he always refused it, anyway. It only made their interaction longer. So, instead, she slightly bowed her head. "Thank you."

"Oh, Eira ..."

Kenji's voice stopped her, and she wondered if today would be the day he had built enough courage to ask her out. It wasn't that there was anything wrong with him, per se, but something about him had her gut flipping into knots. It was probably because everyone avoided her at all costs, so him being interested had her telling herself there must be something wrong with him.

He nervously stared at her for a few moments before he simply just waved. "Have a good day!"

Thankfully, it wasn't, she thought, waving back. "You, too."

She headed back home; it was still early when she almost made it to the front door. The sun was still shining beautifully, so much so she didn't think her grandmother's bones could possibly be right, making her feel sad that her grandmother really was getting that old. So, she decided to head up the little trail she had started to create with her own footprints over the years.

Eira hiked up the mountainside toward the only place on this earth that made her feel truly safe. You wouldn't think so by looking at it, as she took a seat on the lush grass at the edge of a treacherous cliff, but it brought a sense of peacefulness to her core. Staring out at the vast world, hundreds of feet high, where the cliff met the drop of the ocean, she suddenly didn't feel so alone.

That was what she was—*a loner*, she thought, lying back on the grass beneath her. *No, a monster.*

She raised her left hand so the sun could shine down on the taut, scorched skin as she twirled it in its rays. Her skin had deeper pink valleys and higher branching veins spanning overtop, like the roots of a tree. The veins had practically turned colorless with time as they glistened in the sun from the burn, taking any little color she actually had in her skin.

As she lay here in the grass, she thought about how some parts of the left side of her body would never tan again. That was one of the things she had loved before the accident—to lie nearly naked in the warm sun, to get sun kissed. But now she lay in it covered almost head to toe, with only her burned hand and face exposed, as they were the only parts that had gotten used to it over time.

It was easier this way, to cover herself completely. Not only was the sun now harsh on her seared skin, but so were people. People were generally unkind, and children unkinder. Especially the ones at the age when she had gotten burned. So, when there had been nothing left for her after she left the hospital nearly a year later but pain, she had decided to move into her grandparents' home.

It was far from where she had grown up, yet not nearly

far enough. Truthfully, there wasn't much farther than the edge of the sleepy little fishing village she now resided in.

Except for maybe there ...

Sitting up on her elbows, she squinted her eyes to view the little, far-off island she could only view from up here that was completely covered in trees. Then, and maybe only *then*, she just might be far enough. For now, her grandparents' home that stood toward the base of the mountain would have to do.

Falling back on the grass, Eira stared up into the blue sky. It looked so vast from up here with nothing in the way to obstruct her view. She could almost reach up and ...

Raising her hand out of the sun-warmed grass, she reached for the clouds. Alas, her arm wasn't long enough to touch them.

With disappointment, she let her hand drop back to earth as her lids became heavy. It might not have been the smartest thing to take a nap on the edge of a cliff, but with her eyes coming to a close, it was rare for Eira to find peaceful sleep ...

The strangest dream lulled in her mind, and she would later swear it felt as real as when she was awake. She was dreaming of herself trapped in another body, one of a scarred girl named Chloe, when the nightmares of another life caused her to jolt awake.

Suddenly rising, she looked out at the edge of the cliff and into the beautiful water that the sun was setting upon, the blue sky now orange. It was a different, breathtakingly beautiful place altogether than when she had fallen asleep.

The fear of the nightmares that weren't hers left her body and only returned at the sudden deep voice she heard from behind her.

"Hey—"

4

HEY, DARLING.

"Hey, darling."

Eira jumped straight up off the ground and to her feet to face the man who had managed to creep up behind her. The sheer fear that coursed through her veins that was bringing out her instinct to fight or flight became muddled when she caught sight of him.

Her need and want for a man might've been dormant, but she knew a good-looking one when she saw one, and this one was easily the most beautiful one she had ever seen on this side, and on the other side, of the earth where she had been born.

Well, she *might* think that about him if he hadn't snuck up behind her with no one around in hearing distance as the sky was beginning to grow dark.

As she was reminded of the fading light, instincts kicked back in, and her chest fell heavily with quick deep breaths as she took a step backward. "Who are you? I've never seen you in the village before."

The beautiful man slightly smiled, preparing to introduce himself as he took his own step, but forward. "I'm R—"

Immediately, Eira had taken another step back, wanting to keep a safe distance from him.

"Don't take another step back!" The man's harmless demeanor and tone quickly changed in a flash. He turned commanding, his voice now alluring, showing her he had simply put on a mask. Holding out a hand, he waved for her to come back. "One more step back, and you'll fall right off this cliff."

Her eyes squinted, trying to adjust to the dimmer light to see him better. She wasn't sure, but he almost looked ... *concerned? Worried? Frightened?* Those words swirled through her mind like the wind that was beginning to swirl around them from the storm brewing off a bit away in the sky.

He, too, clearly felt the wind picking up, as the concern —or whatever it was—grew on his fierce features. "Look, darling—"

"Eira." She didn't know why it mattered, as she was one step away from death, but she corrected him all the same.

"Look, *Eira*," he tried again, this time softer, more soothingly, "how about I take a few steps back, if you do the same forward?"

She thought for a moment. It wasn't the fear of falling to her death that scared her in this moment, but the unknown, breathtakingly beautiful man. Yes, he was stunning to look at, but the more she did so, the more he frightened her. His dark eyes practically glowed the more the sun faded, as if he somehow had night vision. But it was the sheer height of him that had her frozen in place. He was far away from her, but even at this distance, she could see how giant he actually was. If he got close enough to grab her

20

before she could figure out if he was good or evil, she was sure he could break her like a twig.

Feeling certain there was nothing behind the heel of her foot but air, she finally gave in. "All right." She swallowed. "You first."

It was like he didn't want to take a step back when contemplation crossed his features like it had hers seconds ago. But why did it look like his conundrum was if he took a step back, then he might not be able to jump after to save her? As if that was somehow possible?

Finally, he nodded, taking a single step. "Okay, now you."

Eira took a step, and then another with him as they moved in sync, her forward and him backward, like a dance, until she was a couple of feet from the edge of the cliff.

"I'm Ryu," he finally announced with a released breath, and it was like the mystery man could finally breathe now, making him even more of a mystery to her despite finally learning something about him.

The way he seemed to look at her was way different than anyone had looked at her after the accident, and even different than how Kenji looked at her. It was similar, as it wasn't out of disgust, but more powerful—*much more* powerful—yet so pure. There was something she doubted in Kenji's eyes that had her flight mode kicking in, and while she was frightened of Ryu, the longer she stood before him, the less she felt the need to run. She would think she might still feel the need to fight, but truthfully, she wasn't much of a fighter, and it was clear there was absolutely no point against him.

Usually, her gut, bones, and all the other matter in her body told her to run from dangerous men. So, why was every cell in her body now telling her she was in the right place at the right time? It wasn't like it wasn't clear that Ryu was, in fact, dangerous, yet her body felt magnetized to his.

She kept her feet steady on the ground, but it wasn't without difficulty, as she internally ached to move closer to him with each passing second.

The question was: *did he feel it, too?*

While her body might be convinced of him, her mind had yet to be.

"Why is it that I've never seen you around the village before, *Ryu*?" She repeated his name as if to commit it to memory.

"I live in the next village over." His eyes wavered, like they were searching for something, until they landed on her tote with the contents of her market run spilling out. "To get supplies."

Okay, now I *really need to run.*

Eira's own eyes searched around for the best escape route, and right when she had decided which way to run, he did something to distract her.

Ryu crouched to the ground, holding his hands out in surrender. "Please, don't run."

Pausing in astonishment, she knew full well she should be booking it back to the house. Instead, she couldn't help herself from asking, "Why are you crouching?"

"I don't know," he admitted in defeat. "I thought I might seem less intimidating down here."

"Well, you're not. It's making it worse. I feel like you're about to pounce on me at any second."

"Sorry, I'm just scared you'll run from me, and then—" He breathed, rising back up ever so slowly, debating on whether he wanted to say his next words. "*And then,* I'll never see you again."

Strangely, it felt like Eira held all the power from the sheer desperation in his voice.

Her chest suddenly became heavy again as she whispered, "Why?"

Ryu thought for several more anguished, breathless moments, still wondering exactly what he wanted to reveal. "If I tell you, then you *really* will run from me."

A knowing chill went down her spine ...

He felt it, too.

5

MAKE NO PROMISES

The rain droplets falling onto her cheeks reminded her that she needed to get going, that her grand-mother was probably getting worried sick about her.

"I really need to get home," Eira announced, quickly picking up her tote and fallen-out contents. Wanting to begin her journey, she was careful to go the long way around him. She thought that might be it between them, which strangely caused her heart to scream out in pain, but then she looked back to see he was following her, keeping the same distance that was already between them. It should have scared the hell out of her, so why did it make her heart sing? "What are you doing?"

"Well, I really can't let you walk home in this storm alone."

"Yes, you can." She had to yell back at him over the rain. "I've walked this trail a million times. I'll be fin—"

Eira fell as fast and as hard as the pouring rain that had suddenly started coming down. She had barely gotten her brain unscrambled before he almost ...

"Don't!" she screamed out in horror.

Ryu had quickly closed the distance and was just about to touch her arm when he halted his hand. Calmly, he spoke in an even, soothing tone, careful not to move another muscle. "I was only going to help you up, I promise."

Eerily, she believed him, but ... "Please, just don't touch me."

"I know we only just met"—the plea in her eyes had Ryu's voice turning soft—"but I can promise you here and now that I wouldn't ever hurt you, Eira."

Again, everything about herself told her to trust him at his vow. However, that wasn't the problem.

"If you don't ever want to hurt me, then swear to me you'll never touch me. *Not even* if I'm falling."

"I ca—" Even through the pouring rain, it was clear in Ryu's fierce eyes that he didn't want to agree to that, but then he backed off. He didn't put the kind of distance that had been there before between them, but he at least gave her a foot, showing her he didn't want to go far. "I swear not to touch you until you ask it of me, *if* you make a promise to me in return."

"*If?*" Not so gracefully, Eira defiantly made it up off her ass, trying to wipe the mud off her hands before giving up to swipe them on her pants. "That's not how it works."

"I can swear not to touch you, but you can't make me promise not to catch you when you fall. If you want me to let you fall on your ass again, darling, then you must promise me something in return."

Eira stormed off through the storm, trying to think just *how* clumsy she was for a moment. How often could she possibly slip—

Shit. She almost just fell flat on her face this time. The laughter coming from behind her wasn't helping her think, either.

What could Ryu possibly want her to promise him? Oh dear, she probably shouldn't want to know.

"All right, fine!" she grumbled, coming to a stop after she barely caught herself this time. The steep land that she loved had betrayed her for the last time. "What is it you want?"

She watched as Ryu came to stand in front of her, towering over her with each closer step, then held her eyes captive.

"Promise me you won't ask me to leave you when we get down this mountain."

Again, the desperation in his voice nearly broke her betraying heart this time. Her mind kept telling her she was supposed to do exactly that, but how could she when the thing in her chest told her she couldn't? It was a desperate battle she had hoped to fight at the bottom, but now it could no longer wait.

"I can't—"

"I know you feel it, darling." The smile that touched his lips became deadly as he watched the drops of rain beautifully fall down the scorched half of her face. He might not have touched her physically, like he obviously wanted to, yet she still felt as if he had with his gaze all the same. "You won't be asking me to leave you by the time we get down this mountain, anyway."

Her breath caught in her throat. *Is he right?* Already, it felt as if her body couldn't imagine a moment without him, even though they had just met moments ago. The feeling was simply inexplicable. So inexplicable that she was beginning to wonder if he had put a spell on her while she'd napped, as the only thing fighting off the spell was her mind and past trauma.

Are witches real, or warlocks, or whatever?

Eira didn't think so. But whatever this was, it was something of legends.

"So, what will it be, darling?" he asked, still sneering.

Giving her own smile, she made him a promise that only she could keep. "Fine. I promise that *I* won't ask you to leave when we get to the bottom of the mountain." *But I make no promises my grandparents won't leave your ass in the rain when we reach my house.*

His strange, glowing eyes slightly squinted at her, as if he sensed a catch, but then he nodded, keeping the agreement they had already made. He even stayed true to his word when Eira took only a few steps forward and met the wet, muddy ground again.

The laughter cutting through the storm might've pissed her off, if it didn't prove just how honest he was.

"Well, at least I know you keep your promises," Eira mumbled under her breath, not even bothering to wipe the mud off her hands this time.

"Always," he assured her.

What the—

She couldn't understand how he could've possibly heard her. Something was definitely *off* about him, but her attention went to his word.

Always.

That word had her heart, which trusted him, practically thumping out of her chest. Her body, which didn't want to leave him, might've been happy, but her mind still couldn't help but think how long exactly he planned to stay with her

...

She tried her best to put it out of her mind so she could make it to her house without a fully black and blue bum in the morning. As she did so, it was weird how quickly she began to relax around him, knowing he wouldn't touch her. All the pressure of when she usually first met a stranger had evaporated.

For once, she felt *free* in the presence of a stranger.

And for once, she finally had trust in someone.

But now, as they reached the base of the mountain, it was time for her mind to finally win out.

Eira had only barely touched the doorknob when it was slung open.

"Where the hell have you been?"

Stepping inside, she felt like a cold, wet dog as she continued to get berated. "Grandma, there's—"

"I told you to be home before the storm!"

"Grandma!" She tried to tell her there was company waiting outside the door, but her grandmother continued.

"I've been worried sick!"

"Ahem," Ryu coughed, letting his presence known.

She suddenly stopped mid-reprimand at the sound, and her grandmother's gaze went to the man still standing in the pouring rain. Then ...

Her mouth dropped open. "Oh my—"

6

STORMS AND DRAGONS

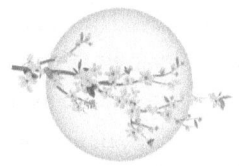

"Hello, I'm Ryu."

She watched him introduce himself sweetly, like he had with her before he revealed his true self. *What a load of garbage.* Hell, Eira was sure she hadn't seen the real, *real* Ryu yet, either. She imagined he had only shown her the tip of the iceberg.

"I met Eira at the market and just wanted to be sure she made it home safely in this storm."

What a double load of garbage.

"Oh." Grandmother tried to pull herself together but was too enamored at the sight of the tall, beautiful man at the door. "How sweet of you to do that for my granddaughter."

"Of course," he said, still getting drenched from the rain as he looked up at the dark sky. "I'm not sure when this is going to let up, but I guess I should start my *long* journey ho—"

"I'm sorry, where are my manners?" Grandmother laughed, a bit embarrassed at herself. "Come inside; you can't possibly walk far in this."

"Thank you." Ryu stepped into the warm, dry home, which had her tiny grandmother backing up at the sheer height of him.

"Oh, my—"

"Is dinner ready yet?" Grandfather asked, followed by the sound of shuffling into the living room.

"Honey"—his wife moved toward with a big smile—"Eira made it home, and look what she brought with her."

Grandfather, who must now be as blind as he was deaf, had completely missed the giant. He had to look up a couple feet to see his face.

Again, Ryu immediately switched on the charm with a slight bow. "Hello, sir. I'm Ryu—"

"Husband," he said with a nod, cutting him off before looking back to his wife and moving on to more important things. "I'm hungry."

"Shoot!" she yelled and ran off as if remembering something. By the smell of it, it was the thing starting to burn. "Come; stay for dinner, Ryu!" she yelled over her shoulder before she disappeared.

With her grandfather following his wife like a starved puppy into the kitchen, Eira looked at an awfully smug Ryu.

"After you," he said with a killer smile and a wave of his hand toward the kitchen.

Rolling her eyes, she stomped off in defeat. She already knew he was going to have her grandmother eating out of the palm of his hand, and he was going to go nowhere tonight. Her only hope was if it stopped raining sometime soon. By the sound of the rain hitting the roof, however, that wasn't likely.

Ryu took up most of the small kitchen when he entered. The fourth chair that usually sat in the corner of the room had been brought up to the table already, and when Ryu took it, he dwarfed the table, taking up that whole side.

Eira began setting the table, and by the time she was finished, her grandmother had served the last dish as well.

"Thank you." Ryu politely bowed. "It looks delicious."

"You're welcome," her grandmother said, taking the seat in between her husband and Ryu.

Eira did the same on the opposite side. She had to scooch closer to her grandfather when Ryu reached to fill up his plate and his big arm almost hit her.

"Wow, it tastes just as delicious as it looks," he complimented after taking his first bite.

Grandmother blushed. "Thank you."

"Suck-up," Eira mumbled under her breath, knowing only he would hear it. The slight smile that touched his lips told her he did.

"So, where do you live?" Grandmother asked once her flush had disappeared.

"Yeah, Ryu"—Eira smirked, just as curious—"where *do* you live?"

"In the next village over," he replied nonchalantly before taking another bite.

"Which one exactly?" she asked, smiling wider, thinking she had him.

Grandfather had just shoveled some rice into his mouth, which had some of it spitting out when he named it.

"Ine?"

Dang it!

"Yep, that's the one." Ryu gratefully took the scapegoat approach.

Unfortunately, Eira had lost her appetite, too deep in thought about the strange man she had let follow her

31

home. Pushing the food across her plate, she wondered where the hell Ryu must have come from because he clearly didn't know the area.

"That is a far journey home. What made you come here?"

Answering her grandmother, he didn't take a second to complete his lie. "I came to get some things from the market that we don't have from home, and that's when I met Eira."

Hearing her name, she finally looked up from her plate at him. It looked as if he had been studying her burns again now that he had better light.

"How lovely," Grandmother swooned before remembering something else. "Oh, Eira, did you get the ingredients for your tea?"

"Yes, it's in my bag on the counter."

"Good." After taking one last healthy bite of her meal, Grandmother began preparing the tea. "So, what do you do, Ryu?"

Conveniently, he had just taken a big bite, which gave him time to clearly think. "I teach martial arts."

"Really?" Grandmother spun around from her concoction to look at him. "Well, I suppose you look like you do."

"Yes." He laughed. "I teach it to some of the children in my village."

Ha! Eira practically snorted, trying to hold in her laughter. She didn't doubt he knew how to fight, but he looked more like an assassin. There was no way in hell he was just a teacher.

"Oh, how sweet!"

She rolled her eyes heavenward again. How someone as sharp as her grandmother could be so easily fooled by him just proved he probably was a witch. *I mean warlock.*

"Here you go." Her grandmother handed her a hot cup of the tea. "I'd offer you some, Ryu, but it will knock you right out."

"What do you mean?" he asked, confused.

"Eira drinks it to sleep. It's about the only thing that gets her to fall asleep these days."

The look she had given her grandmother to shush clearly hadn't worked.

Softly blowing on the hot liquid, she caught Ryu staring at her again, but this time, it wasn't at her burns but her lips.

"I see," he said, clearing his throat. "Yeah, I wouldn't want to take that, considering I have a long walk ahea—"

"Oh, nonsense," Grandmother hushed him. "You're not going anywhere tonight, not in this storm, you're not."

"It's okay. I don't want to intrud—"

Pfft. Yeah, righ—

As if right on cue, lightning struck hard with a flash, followed by a thunderous bang.

"Well, if you don't mind?" he asked.

"Of course not." She nodded, confirming his stay.

Finally full, Grandfather shook his head and mumbled at the next strike of lightning, "Dragons."

"Dragons?" Ryu asked curiously, wondering if he had heard him right.

"You haven't heard the old wives' tale about storms and dragons?" Grandmother was the one to ask as she finally started looking at him like he had been living under a rock.

"No." Ryu shook his head. "I can't say that I have."

"Well," she continued, "on stormy nights like this, they say it's dragons fighting."

He simply said one word.

"Interesting."

7

DON'T LOOK AT ME LIKE I'M THE WEIRD ONE

L ooking at the abnormally large black eyes, she was sure she was looking into the eyes of the devil.

The silver blade inched closer and closer to her right eye until it was mere centimeters from her pupil.

"Don't blink."

A tear welled up in her eye, making it even harder to keep her eyes open. Her body began to tremble. She was going to blink.

"Don't blink, little girl," he warned again.

The tear fell, and her eyes started to close ...

"Eira ... Eira ... Eira!"

The lulling sound of her name getting louder brought her back to this universe.

"Don't touch me!" she screamed, jolting herself awake. Eira sat up, bundling her blanket around her in an attempt to safely be cocooned from the dark figure of the man standing over her.

The figure reached over, turning on the soft glow of the

lamp on her bedside table. "I promised you I wouldn't touch you, and I didn't."

Her racing heart began to steady at seeing it wasn't the devil's dead black eyes who haunted her sleep staring back at her, but Ryu's warm, glowing ones. She checked her right eye to see it was perfect, then her left to feel the imperfection of the burns surrounding it. She was safely back in her body.

His jaw flexed in a tight clench. "It wasn't without difficulty, though."

"You really didn't touch me, did you?" she whispered in disbelief that he kept his promises so fiercely.

"Trust me." Running his hand through his disheveled hair in anguish, he sat down on the edge of her bed, trying to calm himself down. "You'd know it if I did, darling."

Eira didn't know exactly what he meant by that, yet she loosened her protective cocoon. It was obvious there was nothing to fear in his presence. Whatever code he lived by was extremely important to him, and she knew she herself was becoming just as important to him with each passing second. She knew it because, like he'd said, she felt it, too. As her heart continued to steady, she noticed his steady alongside hers.

"You scared the hell out of me, Eira." Ryu didn't try to hide the agony he had gone through while she was under and screaming. "I've never seen anyone have a nightmare like that."

Still remembering the way those soulless eyes had made her feel and the touch of the cold blade piercing above her eye right before she had awoken, she shook her head, wishing she could forget it. "I'm not so sure it was."

He looked at her strangely.

"Oh, come on. Don't look at me like *I'm* the weird one!"

she cried before shivering at the chill that ran up her spine. "I've just never had a nightmare like that."

"What do you mean?" he asked, softening his features so she wouldn't think he was judging her.

Eira didn't know how much she wanted to reveal, yet she wanted him to understand. "Usually, my nightmares are always the same, but this one was different ... like it wasn't mine."

"And how often do you have these nightmares?" he asked after his eyes had drifted to the cup of tea her grandmother had given her earlier in the night. She had barely made it to bed and had taken the last sip before she passed out while her grandmother made a bed on the couch for him.

She thought for a moment, remembering the one from earlier in the day. "I-I actually had one earlier when I fell asleep on the mountain, but that was the first time."

"And what are yours about?" he asked softly, wondering about the nightmares she usually had.

Now Eira didn't know what to say. What was she was supposed to tell him? That every time she closed her eyes, nightmares of the past haunted her so much that she'd rather suffer not sleeping at all most nights? *Yeah, right.* All she needed was for him to think she was a monster, like everyone else did.

"It's your fault!" she realized, saving her from the subject. "You're the reason I'm having these dreams that aren't mine."

"*My fault*?" It was clear he took offense.

"Yes, your fault," she reiterated, knowing it was true. "Because each time I've had one, I've woken up to you staring at me. And don't try to tell me it's a coincidence, because coincidence, I think not—"

"I wasn't going to," he answered, as if deep in thought now.

"Oh." Clearing her throat, she did some softening herself. "W-why do you think that is?"

"I'm not sure," he answered honestly, still trying to figure it out. "But I'm sorry if I am causing it."

Reading the worry on his face, she hadn't meant for him to feel bad. "It's okay. I'll be all right."

"When we go back to my village, I think I know someone who can help."

Eira blinked back at him. "When *we* go back to your village?"

"Yes." He nodded like it was already a done deal.

"And where is that?" She couldn't bite back her sarcasm. "Ine? Where you teach martial arts to sweet little children?"

Ryu cleared his throat. "I *do* to teach martial arts to children."

"Sure, you do." She laughed, unconvinced. Ryu's code simply made him a terrible liar. "Are you at least going to tell me the name of the village you really live in?"

"Nope." Standing up, he reached for the lamp to turn the soft glow back out. "I'm going to show you."

"Sure, you are." She laughed, convinced he had fallen from the sky at this point. She only stopped laughing when she sneezed.

"Bless you."

"Are you"—following his voice and squinting in the dark to see his voice had come from the floor, she could barely make out he had moved the blankets and pillow her grandmother had placed on the couch for him, to sleep right outside her bedroom door—"sleeping on the floor?"

"Yes," he replied unapologetically.

"Were you sleeping there before?"

"Uh-huh." Still no remorse in his tone.

Eira just shook her head in the dark, knowing it was pointless to talk him back into sleeping on the couch. Again, her mind tried sending alarm bells that the strange man was now sleeping right outside her door, but her heart simply warmed as she snuggled deeper into her bed. "Well, could you at least close the door?"

"Not a chance." Ryu rested his own head softly on his pillow. "Good night, darling."

She only hoped the smile that touched her lips couldn't be heard in her voice. "Night, Ryu."

8

TOO STUNNED TO SPEAK

Death.

That was how Eira felt when she awoke. For once, she had slept without dreams, but she knew it had been too good to be true as soon as she felt the tingle in the back of her throat.

"*Ahh—*"

Oh, no.

"*—choo.*"

Thankfully, Ryu must have closed the door sometime. She hoped her grandmother hadn't heard her sneeze through the thin walls, but she knew that was also too good to be true when she heard a knock on her door.

"Eira, honey, are you all right? It's almost noon."

Desperately, she tried sitting up to look alive, but her grandmother was already flinging open the door.

"Almost noon?" she asked, hoping she didn't sound as bad as it had felt to speak.

The look on her grandmother's face told her it did. "Oh, no, no, no, no."

Still, she tried to play it off, getting out of bed.

"No, you're not going anywhere." Grandmother pointed a strong finger at her to keep her in place.

"Really, I'm fi—ahh-choo."

"Is everything all right?" Ryu asked, appearing out of thin air at the door like he lived here now.

"No, it is not. Eira got herself a cold from the rain." Grandmother began her scolding again as she carefully tucked her back into bed without touching her. "I told you it was going to storm and to get back, but you never listen to me."

With a serious look, Ryu walked into the room. His eyes scanned her complexion, and it wasn't in the way they did before when he'd studied her scars; it was with concern and concentration. "You look like you're running a fever."

"You could always tell with her cheeks," Grandmother agreed.

"I'll get you some water," he said right before leaving.

She tried pushing back the blanket again, knowing what was coming. "I feel okay, Grandma; I promise."

"Nope, you need to stay right here till it passes."

That was what Eira had been afraid of. She could stay in her bed when she was sleepy and night came, but she hated it during the day, knowing what demons always waited in her sleep. She had been grateful every morning to leave it and dreaded when the time came for her to enter it. To stay here all day for consecutive days was, for lack of a better word ... a nightmare.

"I'll head to the market to get you some medicinal tea."

"I can go," Ryu offered, returning with a glass of water.

"Shouldn't you be on your journey home by now?" Eira asked, giving him a not so subtle hint.

"Eira!" Grandmother scolded her of being rude before

turning to Ryu. "That is so nice of you to offer. It's hard for me to make it to the market these days."

Ryu smiled, unbothered by Eira's words. "Of course. I don't mind at all."

"I'll go make a list of the things you need to get."

Eira's eyes turned into slits at him when her grandmother turned her back, and she waited until she disappeared into the kitchen before she spoke. "What are you doing?"

"Going to the marke—"

"No." Eira gave him a look. "*What are you doing*?"

"Let me make this easy for you." Ryu took a seat on the edge of her bed again, making himself comfortable. He then lowered his mask a bit more. "I am not leaving without you, Eira. Once you're better, you *will* be going back home with me. So, get used to me, darling—you're going to see a lot of me."

With each word he spoke, Eira's mouth had dropped further and further. Right when she gathered enough of her thoughts, she went to speak, but Grandmother's voice could be heard yelling from the kitchen.

"Ryu!"

When a now satisfied Ryu got up to leave at his cue, Eira tried to find her voice again.

"Shh, darling," he shushed her rather lovingly. "You're too sick to speak. Drink your water and feel better. I'll be back soon."

Too sick to speak ... Eira's mouth only dropped somehow more as she watched him walk away proudly.

... try too stunned to speak.

Grandmother's medicine for any kind of sickness, no matter what it was, was first, strict bedrest, and then a small cup of her "medicinal" tea every three hours that might as well have come from the depths of hell. Eira didn't know what all was in it, and she'd rather not ever know, because there was no way in hell she would ever have plans of making it.

"Here you go, honey." Grandmother placed the cup on her bedside table, waking Eira back up.

She hadn't even realized she had passed back out; the sickness was really starting to take over now.

"Thank you, Grandma."

"You know, that boy is going to come in handy. It's been a long time since we had a strong man able to work around the house." She smiled widely, her mind clearly running rampant with all the chores a tall Ryu could do.

"Um …" Eira started to say as her jaw dropped to the floor yet again. "Grandm—"

But she was already running back to the door, not even hearing her contest. "Get some rest, Eira."

The door slamming shut had a dumfounded Eira left with nothing to do but pick up the piping-hot tea. She downed the gross liquid and made a grotesque face.

That was only the first cup, and it was always the easiest to stomach. It all quickly went downhill from there. Only one thing could give her pleasure out of this …

Please let Ryu get sick, too.

Crack.

The sound of broken bones greeted her ears as a baseball bat slammed down onto a limp body.

Snap.

Another flash of the bat making contact with the man's leg, the man who lay practically lifeless on the floor.

He raised the bat once more, pausing only to look her in the eyes. An evil pair of blue-green eyes stared back at her, making her blood run cold.

She watched his hands grip the neck of the bat with a force so intense she was positive it was going to shatter before the bat was brought down for its final time.

Crunch.

As she watched the man inhale the air around him, he looked crazed, his appearance disheveled. Then he slicked his overgrown hair back in place, and you could see the slight smile come to his lips ...

"Eira ... Eira?"

Again, her name being called lulled her out of her nightmare.

"You had another one again, didn't you?" Ryu asked, taking a deep breath.

Now that the sun had gone down, she only knew it was Ryu because she had committed his voice to memory. It took her a moment to be able to see him, and once she did, she could read the growing worry on his features because she was dreaming these dreams that weren't hers. Seeing the guilt, knowing he had caused it, hurt her heart that had already been won by him. Thankfully, the rest of his appearance gave her a chance to change the subject seamlessly.

"Why are you filthy?"

"I did some outside work for your grandmother."

By the look of him and his clothes covered in dirt, she didn't doubt it. Eira could only imagine the work his grandmother had put him to. She had been asking Grandfather to do some work on the outside of the house for years now.

Taking the hot tea he held out to her, she looked down at the gross steamy liquid. "How do you feel? Are you sick?" she asked, maybe a bit too hopefully.

Ryu laughed, his tenseness from her dreams finally easing up. "No, I don't get sick."

"What do you mean, you don't get sick?" she asked, taking the cup away from her mouth and stopping before the liquid had hit her lips.

"I've just never been sick." He shrugged like it was no big deal.

"Never been sick?" she reiterated in disbelief. "How does that even happen?"

Ryu smiled. "Magic."

9
WHO'S KENJI?

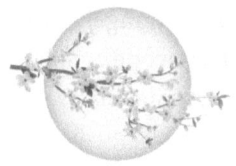

"Eira, you're still sick. Get back in bed."

She slumped down on the kitchen table in defeat. She was so tired but couldn't stand her bed for another second. "Please, no."

"Look at you; you look like crap."

Gee, thanks. One thing about her grandmother ... she was way too honest at times.

"You didn't sleep at all, did you?" she continued.

"I—*ahchoo*—couldn't after sleeping all day!" Eira snapped, a bit from irritableness, and the sneeze didn't help. Truth was, she couldn't after that last dream she had about the man with those blue-green eyes. He was different than the first man she had dreamed about. That one had, for some reason, reminded her of the devil, like he dripped pure evil out of every pore and was just a straight-up psychopath with a knife. But this new one ... was different altogether. He looked *almost* perfectly normal, alluring even, and definitely too handsome for his own good. It was like you wouldn't recognize he was crazy unless he had a reason to show you. Those were the truly scary ones, because you'd go out of your way to cross to the opposite side of the street so you wouldn't cross paths with the first one, but the one with the weird-colored eyes, you'd walk right past him and hope you caught his attention. That and the fact he beat a man in cold blood with a bat was what made him so dangerous.

It also felt as if she strangely knew him, or maybe he just reminded her of someone ... She just didn't know who or why she was having someone else's dreams.

"Please don't make me go back to that room. I just need ..." Eira didn't know what to say to get out of returning to her room, afraid that the next time she accidentally fell asleep, her dreams would be worse. "I need ..."

"Some fresh air?" Ryu suggested, entering the room.

"Yes, some fresh air would be nice," she agreed, grateful for the suggestion. And if she hadn't been so grateful, she'd ask why the hell he was still here.

Grandmother shook her head, looking at the state of her, which made her only feel weirdly self-conscious in front of Ryu. "No, you need rest."

Eira abruptly stood, ready to storm out.

"I think some fresh air might be what she needs. It's sunny, and some vitamin D would do her some good. I can go with her and make sure she's back soon."

Grandmother thought about Ryu's offer for a few moments. "Fine. You can walk to the market and get more root for your sleepy tea that *I will* be making for you as soon as you get back," she scolded.

Already? Either Kenji really had been stingy this time, so she'd come back, or Grandmother had been putting it in her medicinal tea.

"Thanks, Grandma." She picked up her tote off the

counter, feeling better already to be released from the confines of the house.

She was almost out of the kitchen when her grandmother opened her too large mouth.

"And tell Kenji I said hello."

It wasn't necessarily what she'd said but how she'd said it. Her tone and smile felt awfully mischievous. There was something there that Ryu undoubtedly picked up on.

"Who's Kenji?"

Ryu's question appeared totally harmless as he led on to be cool, calm, and collected, but for some reason, she could feel the heat beginning to radiate underneath his skin. It was like a fire had suddenly been set ablaze in the room, and all Eira wanted to do was run from it.

"Oh, just a cart boy at the market who has a big fat crush on Eira," Grandmother revealed with a wink at her granddaughter.

Ryu picked up an apple out of the wire basket that sat in the middle of the kitchen table and inspected it before shining a dirty spot out on his shirt. "Oh, really?"

"No, he does not!" Eira snapped back at her grandmother, feeling her cheeks get hot out of embarrassment, or the continued heat that radiated from Ryu's direction.

"Hush." Grandmother waved her off. "He does, too, and you know it."

Okay, fine, she did know it, but for some reason, she didn't want Ryu knowing it. She just wanted the fire that was rising inside of him to be smothered.

This time, her voice was a bit smaller as she helplessly lied, "Does not."

Ryu took a vicious bite out of the apple. His tone felt poisonous when he said, "I guess I'll be the judge of that."

"All right, great. Time to leave," she muttered under her

breath before running out this time. She kept running, right out of her home and down the path, toward the market, needing to desperately get away from Ryu's warmth that was starting to make her sweat.

"Slow down, darling," Ryu said, catching up. "I didn't think you'd be in a rush to get back home."

Dammit. Eira slowed, knowing he was right. Taking a few calming breaths, she focused on the cool breeze blowing on her skin.

"Are you okay?" he asked in concern.

"Yes, I just got too hot." Still feeling suffocated, she rolled her long sleeves up to her elbows in an attempt to cool down.

Ryu didn't miss the burn scars that trailed all the way up on her left arm until they disappeared under her sleeve. Swallowing hard, his jaw flexed, now understanding. "You don't like to get hot because of the burns."

There was no point in confirming his assumption, because they both knew the answer.

"We can go back—"

"No," Eira stopped him, pleading to continue on their journey. "I can't go back to my room anytime soon."

"So, you did have another dream," Ryu confirmed his thoughts from yesterday. However, instead of making her turn back, he continued walking and went back to eating his apple, giving her some relief.

Having the subject changed helped to cool her almost instantly.

"I ... did," she admitted, unable to lie to him.

The silence that came over Ryu when he tossed his core to the ground frightened Eira a bit as they continued side by side. She couldn't help but wonder what he was thinking, as she could see he was deep in thought.

Feeling like she should have lied, she made a silent promise to herself just to lie to him next time he asked. Making Ryu unhappy killed a part of her.

She desperately tried to figure out what to say to stop his mind from going a mile a minute, but she only had one thing to say when the market finally came into view.

"Any chance you'll stay here and just let me get the root?" she hoped while pulling out a tissue from her pocket to blow her nose.

Ryu simply shook his head. "Not a chance in hell, darling."

Dang it. That was exactly what she was afraid of as he took off.

Trying to be the one to catch up to him now, as his strides were about two times as long as they were before, she thought, *Maybe I can just pretend he's not here today. Ryu doesn't know what he looks lik—*

"Hi, Eira!"

Uh-oh.

IO

BETROTHED TO YOU

S
he cleared her throat nervously as she walked up to
the cart. "Hello, Kenji ... Grandmother says hi."

The sweetest smile crossed his lips. "Tell her I
said hello back, of course."

"I will." She sniffled, thinking it might not be so bad
after all as Ryu just stood there, watching the harmless
exchange.

"Oh no, Eira. Are you not feeling well?"

"I'm fine."

Holding out the small root for her to take, he continued,
"Well, you don't sound too well. After work, I could bring
you some of my spicy soup. It really helps clear out the
sinu—"

"She's good," Ryu assured him, snatching the root from
his clammy little hand before Eira could take it. "This is it?"
Ryu asked, holding up the pathetic root before throwing it
down on the cart. "I think it might be more beneficial if you
gave Eira *several* big roots at a time."

A stunned Kenji took several moments to gather
himself. "S-sure."

Eira, who was in just as much shock, watched as Kenji fumbled to wrap a few newer and larger roots together while he attempted to make small talk with Ryu.

"I'm sorry. I don't think we met. Who—"

"Ryu," was the only information he offered to give, and Kenji took the hint.

"H-how's this?"

"Well, it's a start," he said, satisfied enough before placing some money down on the cart. Then he dropped the bundle into Eira's tote.

Kenji shook his head. "That's okay. It's always on the house for Eira."

He didn't bother picking the money back up. "In my village, men aren't allowed to give single women gifts unless they're betrothed."

"Ryu," Eira nervously stepped in. "Kenji's just being nice."

He didn't dare take his eyes off the cart owner as he made himself clear, "Eira will no longer accept gifts from you or any other man in this village moving forward. If you dare to offer her another gift, either in or out of my presence, your family will find your body buried next to your roots."

What the—

Wishing the ground would swallow her whole, she didn't know whether to follow behind Ryu as he started walking away, apologize profusely to Kenji, or simply run in the other direction.

However, when Kenji got out from behind his cart, he approached her. "Eira, are you okay?"

Her instincts had her backing up right as he reached out to touch her.

"I don't think you should be going anywhere with

him—"

Suddenly, before Kenji could finish his sentence, he was grabbed by the back of his shirt, spun around, and his face met Ryu's fist.

"Ryu!" Eira screamed.

She swore she saw him rear his fist back again, but her shrill must've stopped him.

With Ryu stomping off and everyone around rushing over, she contemplated what to do.

As she studied poor Kenji on the ground, holding his bloody nose, she figured he looked *okay-ish?* Well, okay considering the punch he took.

"Sorry, Kenji," she apologized quickly then made it out of there before she was completely surrounded. There were going to be plenty of people to help him, and she knew he would be all right. *Right?* Well, she hoped he would and that he would somehow forgive her in the future.

Trying to desperately catch up, she yelled out his name for him to stop. "Ryu!"

"Eira, I need a minute!" he yelled back over his shoulder, showing no signs of stopping.

It was only getting harder and harder for her to catch up to him, so much so she actually lost him. When she reached the house, she instinctively knew he hadn't entered. Instead, she realized exactly where he must've gone. So, she dropped her tote by the front door before climbing the mountain as fast as she could. She had no signs he had actually gone this way until she finally reached the top of the cliff where they had first met. There, Ryu stood at the very edge, taking several deep breaths.

Eira stayed several feet away, just staring at his back. "You didn't need to do that to him. He's harmless."

"Yeah, right," he scoffed, still staring out at the ocean.

"Kenji is nice, and you're just being jealous."

Ryu spun on his heels and, in what seemed like a single stride, he closed the distance between them, forcing her to face his fury. "He's playing you, Eira. That man is neither nice nor harmless. He knows exactly what he's fucking doing!"

Unafraid, she practically laughed in his face at the thought of someone thinking of Kenji like that. "What ...? By giving me a free root every few days? Yeah, he's a mastermind."

"You're not from this side of the world, darling. He's giving you the gift of a root, symbolizing the relationship he hopes to grow with you one day."

Eira hadn't thought about that perspective.

"Yeah, think about it." His tone dripped with smugness, knowing she knew he was right.

She angrily changed the subject when he turned and went back to staring out at the edge of the cliff again. "Yeah, well, half of me is from this side of the world, too, you know."

"Not the half that was raised here, Eira." Ryu wanted her to understand the difference. "As a child, you are taught certain things about our culture, and once you reach adulthood, you are just expected to know them."

"That's not my fault, Ryu."

"Didn't say it was. But next time, when I tell you something about how this side of the world works, maybe you'll listen to me."

Wishing she had never changed the subject in the first place, she got back to the issue at hand. "You know, even if Kenji is as smart as you think he is, it still doesn't excuse what you did."

The thought of him only set Ryu off again. "He's lucky I

didn't shove my foot up his—"

"What is your deal?" she cut him off, having heard enough. "If I want to accept more roots from Kenji, I am allowed to do so. I'm not—"

When Ryu suddenly spun back to her, she could feel the sheer heat that bounced off his skin. "You accept anything from him for free ever again, I will fucking kill him. Do you understand me, Eira?"

Eira didn't know why or how she found the courage to do so, considering she knew Ryu fully meant what he had just said, but she finished what she was going to say before he interrupted her. "I'm not *betrothed* to you, Ryu." She softly emphasized the word he had used earlier. It actually, and oddly, hurt her heart to say it, and she could see her words had struck him to the quick as well.

As she stared up at a fiery Ryu, she could swear she could see fire burning behind his dark, glowing eyes, and the smile that suddenly lifted his lips sinisterly sent a chill up her spine, even though she was burning from the heat of him.

He reached out to her, letting a single finger get danger-ously close to the burned side of her face as it hovered only a few centimeters above her scarred skin. "I could touch you, you know ..."

She stood there, as still as a statue, as her breath caught in her throat, wanting both to not be touched and, for the first time, to be touched.

I swear not to touch you until you ask it of me.

The words he had said to her at their first meeting were already beginning to come true while her body screamed out for him to finally touch her.

It was nearly impossible not to compare it to Kenji almost touching her and how she had recoiled as she stood in front of Ryu, secretly hoping he would, as she continued listening to him.

"One touch, and you'd think twice about what you just said," he told her hoarsely as his finger traveled over her skin without contact until he went lower and picked up a strand of her hair to twirl it around his finger.

Eira had to close her eyes, unable to look at him teasing her any longer. It was the anticipation of him doing so that was starting to kill her.

He slightly tugged the strand, causing her to close her eyes even tighter.

"Then this game I've been letting you play would be over."

"What?" she breathed.

When she didn't get a response after a moment, she finally opened her eyes back up to see he was no longer there. Nothingness stood in front of her, and when he had left, she hadn't even felt so much as a breeze or her hair fall back to her shoulders.

Mystified, she called out for him, "Ryu?" She spun around in desperation to look for him, tried again louder, her heart already sinking, "Ryu?"

When she still received no response, she carefully went to the edge of the cliff, not knowing why she looked down.

The way the cliff curved down back into the mountain, she could only see waves crashing in the open ocean. She didn't know what she expected to see, anyway, as she hadn't even heard so much as a splash.

Trying once more in sheer hopelessness, her heart cried out his name, but this time she already knew she still wasn't going to receive a response. "Ryu ..."

The strange thing was, it already felt like it had all just been a dream.

II

Nine Petals Remained

Ryu entered the bedroom window without making a sound. Earlier, at the mountaintop, he had just needed a moment to get himself under control, fearful of changing next to her. He was certain if she saw him in his other form, she would never let herself get close enough to touch him, and all would be lost.

As he sat on the bed beside the sleeping beauty, he couldn't believe the woman before him was actually made for him. She was unlike anything he had ever seen, as he had only heard about women who had her features in tales.

He had been carefully studying her over the last few days and the way she covered her scars with her clothes and her veil of hair. She probably thought her burned skin was why people stared at her, but she was wrong. They stared because her beauty wasn't from this side of the earth.

When he heard the lulls of sleep, he could sense the nightmare beginning. If he hadn't made that forsaken promise to her, he would touch her, and this all would be a bad dream in itself. But he had, and he was determined to keep it. Also, his pride wanted her to choose him out of choice and not magic.

He sat there for a few moments, wondering if he should save her from the nightmare that was turning worse by the second. That only, in turn, made him feel worse by the second as well. Ryu didn't have to wake her to know she'd lie about having the dream, as she didn't want him to feel bad about it. They both knew he was causing them. Him sitting down beside her only proved that to be so, as she had been sleeping peacefully until he entered.

Having made up his mind about what he should do, he stood up, leaving the way he had come in. However, when he closed the window, he did it rather loudly and was satisfied when the glow of her bedside lamp turned on.

Where he was going, she wasn't strong enough yet. This, he needed to do alone.

Ryu stared up at the barren Sakura tree. The pit in his stomach at seeing it this wilted frightened him for his village's future.

I haven't been gone that long, have I?

When he'd left, a quarter of the pink leaves had remained. But now, only nine petals remained, hanging on for dear life. He was frightened to even breathe, afraid it would cause some more to fall.

The connection the two beings shared was almost gone. He was able to feel the tether between them stronger when he placed his calloused hand on the trunk of the tree. He felt as if he not only let the magical sapling down, but his father and the whole village.

His pride of letting Eira choose was costing him everything, but he couldn't imagine going back to her and breaking his promise, either.

With footsteps approaching behind him, he could practically hear the disappointment before he even spoke. "You're back, *and without a fated mate.*"

Ryu cleared his throat before looking back at his father, facing him, knowing nothing he was about to say would go well.

"I found her."

"You did?" Relief flooded his older features before revelation finally dawned. "Ryu, why is the tree still dying, then?"

"I—" He didn't know what to say, knowing his father would never understand. "She's special, Father. I can't ..."

"Touch her?" he asked, like it was hard. The disappointment in his voice wasn't because of his son but in himself, as he felt responsible for not letting Ryu leave the village. Now all the blame was put on his son's shoulders. "You simply touch the girl, son. I would have thought that would be easy for you. What does her being special have anything to do with that?"

"It's not that easy," he stated, his fear that his father would never understand confirmed. "She's been hurt in the past. I don't want to be the cause of any more pain."

Tatsu knew exactly what he meant. "No, your pride wants you to talk her into bed, which I'm sure you need time to do with a girl like that. But time is a luxury you don't have—*none of us have.*"

Ryu stood there, unable to find the words. His father's disappointment was not only valid but harsh to take.

As if on cue, a precious bloom began to fall, dancing in the wind to the ground.

"I wondered why the cherry blossoms suddenly started to fall so fast. It's because you found her and are practically mocking the gifts we receive." A displeased Tatsu couldn't even look at his son anymore as he started to walk away. "Is your pride worth the village? Or maybe it's your pride wanting you to be the last Tei so the songs that will be sung of dragons all mention your name."

He violently shook his head, unbelieving his father would even say something so blasphemous. "That isn't true—"

"*Prove* it ..." his father hissed as another cherry blossom fell.

Alone, Ryu stood, looking up at the dying tree in defeat.

Seven remained.

"Come in," he heard her say when he approached the open door.

Entering, he found the old seeress sitting at the small table with a smile on her face.

"Pretty little thing, isn't she?"

"Yes," Ryu agreed, sitting down across from her. "Did you know she was so close?"

"Perhaps." The twinkle in her blind eyes sparkled. "But Eira wasn't ready to be found yet."

"And ..." He swallowed nervously, knowing time was of the essence. "Is she now?"

The old witch cackled. "Well, you found her, didn't you?"

"Yes, but she's afraid to be tou—"

"I warned you she was broken," she cut him off. "That you *both* were."

Ryu didn't need to be reminded of that, even though he didn't feel broken at all.

"How am I supposed to touch her, then?"

Reaching over, she patted his hand to assure him, "In time."

"I don't have time," he said in frustration, smacking his fist down on the table. "There are only a few leaves left."

"Is that why you came here, then? To see how much time you have?"

"No." He calmed himself. "I came because of Eira's nightmares."

She raised an unruly brow. "Oh?"

When she didn't appear to know what he was talking about, he continued, "She told me she's having nightmares that are not hers."

Itako thought for several moments, mumbling as if she were listening to something around her, but Ryu didn't hear anything.

Getting up, the blind lady scurried around the place as if she could see perfectly. When she opened up cabinets, it appeared she was looking for something while she continued to talk to herself.

"What is it? What does it mean?" he asked, standing to follow her around once he realized she knew something.

"You and Eira are soulmates," she began as she carried on looking. "When you met, you must've sparked memories of her past life."

Confusedly, he asked, "Why her and not me?" When she went quiet and didn't want to answer, he growled out, "*Why?*"

Itako stopped, giving him her full attention. Her blind

eyes met his as she told him honestly, "She must've experienced a painful event or death in that life."

It felt as if he had been hit in his chest, knocking the breath out of him.

"The spirit of your dragon must've met her on the other side."

His words were hoarse. "The spirit of my dragon?"

"You not only carry your soul, but the souls of all your ancestors that were dragons before you. My guess is they protected her, assuring that her soul was placed correctly to continue your lineage," she explained.

He looked down at the creaky floor; it was bittersweet to know his ancestors had made Eira possible for him, but it bitterly hurt to know she might have suffered.

"I see."

Itako reached for his hand, taking it in her withered ones. "Her past life doesn't define what could happen in this one," she assured him before placing a small bottle in his hand. "Have her take a drop of this before bed to sleep. She won't dream, and I have reason to believe when you are mated, the dreams will stop ... hopefully."

"Thank you." He nodded his head in understanding of the instructions. "But if our past lives don't define us, then why are we broken in every one?"

"It is cold." The seeress pretended to shiver. "Do you mind getting me some kindle to start a fire?"

"Sure." Swallowing hard, he placed the bottle in his pocket before leaving. He knew she had only requested him to pick up twigs to spare him of the answer.

Fearing that Eira might end up like his mother as he gathered the supplies, he realized how strong his father must be to continue life without his fated mate. While he and Eira had only just met and were yet to be mated, he was certain he couldn't live a single moment in this life without her.

Entering the old place once again, he saw Itako rocking in her chair by the fireplace as she smoked a pipe.

"Thank you," she said, blowing out her words with a puff.

Bending down, he began starting the fire for her when she asked, "Could you hand me a stick?"

Ryu nonchalantly held out a stick, knowing even though she was blind, she'd know where it was. "Here."

"Do me a favor?" she asked, not taking it. "Break it."

Ryu snapped the long, skinny twig in two.

Leaning forward, she pushed his hands together, making him grab the now two sticks together as one. "And again?"

When he went to snap the twigs again, this time it didn't break. Instead, they bent together.

The witch rocked back in her chair, pleased. "Do you understand now, Ryu?"

"Yes, Itako," he said, smiling with relief.

"You are not meant to rule as a broken king, but as an unyielding one with Eira by your side. That is the only thing that remains certain in each of your lives. The rest is determined by fate." She puffed her pipe strongly, and the flame grew brighter. "You can be one of the greatest Tei kings in dynasty history because of this."

The wetness spilled out of eyes and hit his cheeks, unbeknownst to him. "I can?" he asked hoarsely, not believing it.

She nodded. "Yes, but you must make what you will of your destiny."

Understanding now, he tried to make light while

wiping his tears away as he went back to starting her fire. "You can see all that, huh?"

"Well—" Itako laughed. "Let's hope."

Laughing with her for a moment made him start to feel better, but he had one last question ...

"My father ..." he started to ask. However, she already knew what he wondered.

"Yes." She puffed an air of smoke. "When he passes, his spirit will travel with you in this life, but when it's your time, your spirit must move on to meet Eira's in the next."

As he finished up, Ryu felt strong enough to finally leave and claim the woman he was born to be with in each and every life.

When he left his village this time, he knew upon his next return that not only would he never get the chance to leave it again, but his arrival would be with his fated mate.

12

A FULL-FLEDGED DRAGON

Eira sat down near the cliff's edge to watch the sun rise. Before Ryu, she felt like this was *her* special place, but after Ryu, she felt like it was *their* special place. She thought maybe if she returned where they had first met and last seen each other, he might come back. But the longer she sat there as the sun traveled the sky, the more hope she lost.

Her instinct had told her that it would all quickly feel like a dream when he had first disappeared and, unfortunately, she had been right. The only proof he had been there was the bonsai tree Ryu had planted for her grandmother in their front yard.

The worst part was her grandparents didn't even ask her where he had gone. She had prepared herself on what to say on the way back home, but when she had mentioned his name, it was as if they no longer remembered him. Ryu was gone, and so was their memory of him.

Feeling as if she had been locked in a bad dream, with only her memory remaining of him, Eira hadn't fought sleep for the first time, hoping to meet him again in her dreams, but she had dreamed of nothing. Well, *almost* nothing. The second she had started to finally dream, she had awoken to a noise before she even knew what it was she had been dreaming about.

Eira didn't know what was worse: to know him only for him to leave, or to have never known him at all.

With all hope lost and the sun set to fall soon, she stood, wanting to keep her promise to her grandmother that she would come home before darkness fell.

It wasn't until she turned from the view of the ocean to walk down her self-made path that she realized he had been quietly watching her.

"Hey, how long have you been there?" she asked.

"Long enough that you should have noticed." Now that he had been seen, he took a step forward. "But you never notice me."

"Are you all right?" A weird tingle went up her spine at noticing just how disheveled he looked. "Kenji?"

Ignoring her question, he continued with what he wanted to say, taking another step forward. "You've never noticed anything I've done for you."

Taking her own step, but backward, she had to remind herself that it was just Kenji. Regardless of his bruised face and bandaged nose that was making him look frightening right now, he wasn't actually scary or dangerou—

"Years. Years!" Kenji began irrationally raising his voice. "I've tried to get you to notice me!"

Quickly, Eira took another generous step back, knowing Ryu had been right about him.

His voice turned dangerously sinister. "But it didn't even take you a day to notice *him*."

Him? Did that mean ...?

"You remember him? You remember Ryu?"

At her soft realization, Kenji started maniacally laughing, now understanding. "Of course! You noticed him because—"

Eira was clearly missing something as he drew out his next few words. He knew something she didn't, but how could he remember Ryu, yet her grandparents didn't?

The look that crossed his features showed how everything clicked into place for him. His finger rose creepily to point right at her. "You're his fated mate."

Fated mate?

Eira swallowed, desperately trying to wet her dry throat, repeating her thoughts out loud this time, "*Fated mate?*"

"He didn't tell you?" He looked amused now. "And by the looks of it, it seems like he might have left you. *You poor little thing,*" Kenji said, flashing a deadly smile when he took another stalking step closer. "Especially if you're asking me if I remember him. That must mean he really is gone."

Her eyes grew big when she read the hunger and determination grow in his. Eira found herself in the same dangerous situation, except this time, she didn't stand in front of Ryu with her heel hanging halfway off the cliff, but Kenji. Instinctively knowing she wasn't going to get lucky this time around, she thought she could make a run for it, yet she knew it might as well be right into his arms. The question was: did she want an easy, quick death or a possible horrid one that would be drawn out by Kenji's desire?

It was the burns on her skin and the look in Kenji's crazed eyes that reminded her that she wouldn't be doing that again. If he took a single step forward, she would accept her fate by just falling back into oblivion.

Thinking he had her, Kenji started to take another step—

"Kenji, don't!" Ryu commanded, coming up from behind them on the mountain. It was clear he must've looked for her at her grandparents' home, and when he hadn't found her, he'd known where she would have gone.

Seeing him, Eira fought the urge to fall back. "Ryu," she quietly cried his name, knowing he would hear it no matter the grave distance and the fact that Kenji stood between them.

All her fears disappeared at once. She knew in her bones that he would save her. Ryu wouldn't let anything happen to her. He had come back.

He came back for me ...

Kenji had a much different response to seeing him. Fear and desperation seemed to swallow him whole as he looked between the two.

Slowly approaching, Ryu began trying to distract him by talking. "I'm sorry I didn't remember you. You've matured these last few years, *Kenshi*."

His jaw flexed at his true name while he took another step toward Eira.

"Think about this ..." Ryu called out, causing Kenshi to cease for a moment. "You know what it would mean for our people if you hurt her."

"*Our* people?" Kenshi screamed back at him disdainfully. "They banished me! I no longer consider them anything but my enemies."

Eira looked between the two, not understanding again.

With no other options, seeing how far Kenshi had turned, Ryu began pleading now, "Just, please, let her go."

"You know I can't, Ryu." Tears streamed down Kenshi's

face, knowing his fate to come. "We both know I'm dead either way."

The second Kenshi took off toward her, Eira closed her eyes, but it was the sound of a roaring monster that had her opening them again to meet a mythical beast she had never believed to be real.

The sight of facing a full-fledged dragon flying straight at her caused Eira's footing to fail.

She wished beginning to fall to her death were the worst part, but it was watching Kenshi getting eaten whole that was.

13

SCALES TURNED TO SKIN

The moment Kenshi had made a run for his fated mate, Ryu had changed into his higher form, knowing it was going to be the only way he would make it to her in time ...

The only way he could save her.

It was half-rage and half-fear that made his dragon roar to life, and there wasn't a single second's thought before he opened his large serpent-like mouth and devoured Kenshi in a single bite.

Swallowing the traitor to his people whole, with no remorse, caused his rage to calm as fear completely overtook him. Not only did it feel like Eira's fate depended on him, but the fate of his whole village.

Soaring off the cliff, he could see she had already fallen quite a ways as his beastly head rushed down the cliffside to catch up with her. He was so close as he stretched out his talons toward her. She was about to hit the water, and since he knew what that impact would do to her, his dragon picked up speed as if every one of his ancestors had infused their strength in him, to help him reach her before it was too late ...

She closed her eyes to welcome death, but it wasn't the water from the ocean below that she met, but a claw-like grip at her sides. Her eyes flashed back open at the horror of being held in the clasp of the dragon. It was possibly more frightening than death to be gripped by the massive beast, so she lay limp in fear of any movement causing being ripped to shreds.

Then, finally, she started to hear it. It was like a hum—no ... a *whisper*.

Eira?

Ryu's voice rang through her head, but that couldn't be possible.

Eira? Concern had his whisper rising. *Eira, are you all right?*

With fear still immobilizing her, she barely got her mouth to speak. "R-Ryu?"

At her own voice, it was like she could feel the beast take a deep breath as it began to soar the sky with better ease.

You're all right, he promised, relief flooding his voice, but Eira couldn't say the same as she lay in its grasp in pure shock.

At first, she could have sworn this all had to be the worst dream of her life, considering they had been pretty crazy lately. But the longer they flew through the sky, the more she realized it couldn't possibly be a dream.

I'm going to set you down gently. Be ready.

That meant …

Eira was softly dropped back to the grass of the cliff that she had fallen from just moments ago as the talons gently opened around her.

That means the whispers of the dragon were …

Standing there, she watched as the dragon magically began to shift—gold scales turned to skin, shrinking until he became the length in size of the dragon's claw, until it fully transformed into a human she recognized. Ryu was, in fact, the beast. The beast that had not only saved her but murdered Kenji in a single bite. The beast that was now walking right toward her.

As soon as Eira went to take a step back, he softly begged, "Please, don't be frightened, Eira. I would never hurt you. You have to know that by now."

His words struck her because she knew them to be true, and as she looked down at her feet, she noticed where he had placed her.

In dragon form, he had dropped her closer to where she was free to run down the mountainside, while he landed himself closer to the edge. The fact that he knew she would probably be scared of him and didn't want her running off the cliff again told her that, along with everything else he had done since the moment they met. But she couldn't help it. Her mind still felt fear. Especially when she had just witnessed what she had.

"You … you killed him."

"I had to," he said, unashamed. "Kenshi would have grabbed you before you fell and, together, you would have fallen twice as fast, and I wouldn't have been able to save you in time."

Eira blinked at his honest answer and decided to rephrase her statement, "You ate him."

"Would you have preferred I breathed fire and possibly burned you alive with him in the process?"

Dumbfounded, she blinked at him again. His brain had clearly considered all the options that hers couldn't have thought in a million years.

"You can do that?"

"Yes." Another honest answer. "So, is that *I ate him* which frightens you or the fact that I can turn into a drago—"

"Both!" Eira shrieked, feeling as if a panic attack could strike her at any moment, but she was ... *calm*? And even more strangely and possibly worrisome—*happy*?

Ryu had come back for her, and as much as her brain still continued to urge her to run for her life, she kept her footing in place as he stepped closer to her. But why was that?

You're his fated mate.

Some of Kenji's last few words echoed in her mind, causing her to ask, "Why did he say I am your fated mate?"

Ryu closed the distance between them until he stood only a few inches away. "Because you are."

"And what is a fated mate?" she dared to ask as he held her gaze so fiercely.

"You were made for me, Eira, and I've been—"

Suddenly, Ryu fell to his knees in pain.

"Ryu, what's wrong?" she asked, falling to the ground with him and looking him over to check for anything visible to cause his pain, but she wouldn't find it ...

It was the invisible string that tied him to his home beginning to sever that caused the excruciating feeling taking over his body. Instinctively, he knew it must mean that only one precious blossom remained.

As he looked at Eira, a tear slipped down his cheek. His dragon form might have touched her, but his human form hadn't, and only then would the sacred tree stop dying. He was closer than ever to her in this form, but he still didn't dare to reach out to touch her, knowing exactly what it was going to cost him, his father, and the people of his village. But that was the cost to gain something as precious as the woman before him. Ryu had made a promise to his *soulmate*, and he planned to keep them in *each* and *every* life.

14

KISSED BY FIRE

It was everything he could do to continue, knowing the petal would fall at any moment now. He was simply *too late.*

He wanted to finish what he had begun to say before the pain had struck him. Eira still needed to hear what he had to say.

"I've been waiting a long time for you, darling."

"Oh," she breathed but was clearly more concerned with his wellbeing. "Ryu, why are you crying?"

"I-I—" He didn't know how to tell her, nor did he think he would ever tell her; he didn't want her to feel responsible for his failures. It was him who had not left his home sooner, at his father's fears. Ryu was his own man, and it was him alone who needed to take sole responsibility for his failures. He could have slipped out of the village and left at any moment. Instead, fear of leaving his home, his village, had kept him from venturing to find his fated mate. If only he had left sooner. What hurt the most was, *she was just right here ...*

"Ryu?" she continued softly when he didn't answer. "What's wrong?"

Another tear fell while he thought of what to say to her. It was a simple act, one that made him almost dismiss the kind action, as it was something a person would simply do when they saw someone sad, but the second her light fingertip touched his tear, the true bond formed between them, her wet fingertip now touching his smooth cheek.

If he thought what he had felt for Eira before was strong ... it had greatly paled in comparison to now.

Every feeling crashed around her at once when her skin met his. It was like everything tied her to the man in front of her, and in a single breath, she knew all at once that she couldn't breathe a single second without him.

Fated mate.

If she didn't understand what that meant before, it was now as clear as the ocean crashing into the cliff.

The strongest feeling she felt at first was love. While she had never been in love, she still could describe the feeling because it was similar yet extremely different to how she felt for her grandparents. People made love more complicated than it needed to be, as it meant you simply cared for someone who you'd do the littlest act for to make them smile. It was possible she had even loved him before this moment, as all she had wanted was for Ryu to smile ... until she touched him.

Then that feeling of love grew tenfold, so intense that heat began to boil her insides. Everything about her suddenly wanted him, needed him, to get so close that their insides burned together in a scorching fire until they melted together as one.

It was the hunger in her eyes that matched his that gave her away.

Like a statue that looked like it had been carved in pain, Ryu stayed unmoving, still holding true to his honor.

"May I touch you now?" he asked like he was desperate for water after walking days in an empty desert and only she could satiate his thirst.

And just like he had promised her she would, she would beg for his touch if it came to it.

Desperate himself to finally touch her, Ryu not only wouldn't make her beg, but he couldn't. He needed her more than the air surrounding them. All he wanted was to satiate the hunger he had felt since the moment his eyes caught her sleeping form. So, when she softly nodded her head for him to touch her, he slowly raised his own hand to cover the delicate one that still rested on his cheek.

Turning into her palm, he placed a light kiss in the center that he was certain sent an electric current through her, as it did him. Then, with the electricity between them rising, he pulled her closer to him, wrapping her in his arms and holding her tightly, taking it all in.

Her sweet scent that smelled of the honey she frequently drank in her tea.

Her soft frame that he was scared of hurting if he held her too tightly.

It wasn't everything he had hoped and imagined.

It was more.

Finally, he was able to run his hand through her hair in the way he had always wanted to, no longer needing to be so precise and delicate so he wouldn't touch her. Finally, he was able to freely let the silky strands run through his fingers.

"You've felt this the whole time, haven't you?" she whispered while tears slid down her own face as she began to cry.

Getting lost in her misty eyes, he returned the favor by wiping away the tears that rolled down her beautiful high cheeks. He could only nod, remembering ...

Ryu had only just flown out of his village and crossed the ocean that separated his village from the outside world when the scent hit him. It was like every instinct had him on high alert as the pheromones of a woman below entered his blood stream.

It was his fated mate, and he knew it.

His magic kept him protected from being seen as he morphed and landed back on the earth in the small village just below. He couldn't believe how close she must have been this whole time.

Following her scent wasn't hard. He just found himself losing his breath in anticipation as he climbed the forsaken mountain. What was she doing up here, anyway?

When he reached the top, he spotted her at once as the sun shined down on beautiful locks of hair that glistened like fire in the sun. The orangey-red hue wasn't a color seen in these parts of the earth, which made him feel as if he was imagining her.

Thinking she must be a visage, he softly approached to find her sleeping peacefully at the edge of the world. Still unbelieving of his luck, he inched closer, wanting to see her face.

And at the first glimpse, his breath hitched in his throat, and he found himself breathless.

The left side of her face had been scorched with the element that ran through his dragon's veins. He stared at the pink and translucent branching veins; she looked as if she had been kissed by fire.

If a mate was ever made for a dragon, it was this one. Now he only needed a name, and a single touch, and then his lineage would be saved ...

Oh, how easy he had thought that was going to be, but fate was a fickle, funny thing. It wouldn't be until he returned to his village that he would know if they had mated before the last cherry blossom fell.

15
CONSEQUENCES

"There?" Eira's mouth dropped open as she looked out at the open sea. "That's where you live?"

"Yes." His eyes smiled amusedly at her. They had yet to leave since their true mating bond had formed.

Eira couldn't believe it as she continued staring out at the little island far away in the distance, covered in trees. Every day, she would sit at the edge of this cliff, looking longingly at the secluded land, and now she understood why.

Her heart had been calling for her to go there. All the while, she had thought it was because her loner heart craved isolation, but that hadn't been the case at all. It was because her heart had instinctively felt her fated mate's presence there, which made her ask, "How did you find me?"

"Your scent."

Astonished, she snapped her eyes back to him. "*My scent?*"

Ryu laughed. "Yes."

For a moment, Eira had forgotten they were still

wrapped in each other's arms. It had felt like second nature, even for a girl who refused to be touched. Now, however, from that comment, she was aware of it and quickly started to feel self-conscious.

He must have known she was beginning to feel that way, because he continued. "As soon as I flew overhead"— Ryu leaned down to her soft neck and inhaled—"I smelled your sweet scent, and I knew."

Eira was the one sitting as still as a statue now as she tried not to melt at the sensations he was creating.

"What can I say?" Ryu said, placing a light kiss on her sensitive flesh. "My dragon form has a good sense of smell." Flicking his tongue out, he took a taste, "*Mmm, honey.*"

Her insides singed from the touch. All she wanted was for her actions to reciprocate his, but ...

As if sensing her turmoil, Ryu pulled back as his face turned serious. It only seemed to take him a single moment to understand why.

His eyes went to her scars, but he didn't just let them caress the markings this time. Lifting a finger, he was finally able to let them travel over the branching, translucent veins before his hand dropped along with his voice. "Someone did this to you."

She could feel the heat radiating from him, and a new fear unlocked that she could awaken the dragon at any moment as she understood something herself.

When Ryu had run hot in the past, it was most likely because he fought turning into a dragon.

Eira was afraid to respond, but her silence told him everything.

Quickly, Ryu stood, beginning to put a safe distance between them.

"Ryu," she cried out to him in hopes to calm the raging dragon inside. "It was forever ago—"

"Yeah, so long ago now that you still can't be touched."

Her mouth snapped closed, because she knew he was right.

She feared it was always going to feel like it had just been yesterday. However, since Eira had met him, she felt like she'd finally started making progress. Before Ryu, she had been stagnant, as if she were always kept in an endless loop being held over the fire that scarred her for life. Anything before she'd met Ryu truthfully no longer mattered to Eira anymore. All she had wanted since sitting in that hospital bed while recovering was to move on. And, for once, she felt like she could. Like she could at last recover and heal her scars. Not on the outside, of course, but on the inside, where it truly counted. Ryu was giving her a reason to move on, and she didn't want *anything* jeopardizing that.

"Ryu, please, just take a breath. You already risked changing once. If you change into a dragon again, someone might see you."

"They wouldn't," he assured her, practically breathing out smoke. "My magic protects me."

She was simply dumbfounded, not by the literal smoke escaping him, but ... "Not everyone can see you when you're a dragon?"

He shook his head. "Only the people born in my village, and you."

She simply couldn't believe it. *What the—*

Suddenly, Ryu laughed after taking a few calming breaths. It was obvious he remembered something. "It's a good thing you were asleep when I left my village and first flew over; otherwise, you would have seen me."

"That would have been a sight." She laughed with him, happy to continue distracting him. It was helping, so Eira drew closer to him. "How come I didn't see you when you left and came back?"

"I left in the middle of the night, when you were sleeping, and I took a boat back. I didn't want to take a chance you'd see me. And *knowing you*, I figured where you'd be. I thought I'd stop by your grandparents' house before I came up in hopes to spare me a trip up the mountain, but of course you were here."

With that explaining it, she slowly reached her hand out to his, lightly letting her fingertips rub over his supernatural skin to soothe him. She could swear she almost felt the scales underneath. "And your magic?"

Ryu began to relax under her touch. "We believe we get our magic from a tree in our village, on the island."

"*We?*" Her eyes grew wide in delight. "There are others like you?"

Ryu shook his head. "I'm the only one. My father used to be able to shift into a dragon, but he lost the ability when I took my first flight." He looked out toward the little island. "I'll tell you more about it when I fly us back home."

Eira immediately stopped her soothing by dropping her hand from his. "That is definitely not happening."

He frowned, his brows drawing together. "What part? The flying or going back to my village?"

She bit her lip as she grew nervous, unable to say the word *both* out loud.

"Eira, I have to return to my village. There's a reason why I was born the way I was. If I don't return, there will be consequences."

She didn't know what to say or do.

"Like you can see me in dragon form"—he nodded

toward the little tree-covered island—"you can see the island my village rests on, but no one else can."

"They can't ..." she whispered, thinking how that could be possible, even though she had just witnessed a dragon. Now that she thought about it, she had never spoken to anyone about the island and just assumed everyone could see it. "But this is a fishing village; how has no one ended up there?"

"The ocean's current *magically* doesn't let it happen."

All she could think of was one simple word as her mind continued to be overwhelmed in this mythical whirlwind —*wow*.

"My village is a safe place, protected from the rest of the world, and if I don't return, it will no longer have that protection."

Eira looked down at the ground. Freedom to the little island was here, like she always dreamed of, but why was she sad now? The time was here, but how was she supposed to leave her grandparents after everything they had done for her?

"It's your grandparents, isn't it?" he muttered solemnly, knowing it was.

She nodded with tears forming in her eyes. How was Eira supposed to choose between her *fated mate* and the *only family* she had left?

16

PAIN & HORMONES

"What is that?" Eira asked as she watched Ryu begin to slowly tip a small vial of clear liquid into her cup of bedtime tea that Grandmother had made.

"It's supposed to keep you from dreaming the dreams that aren't yours." When a single drop fell, he put the stopper back on then slid the precious liquid back into his pocket before handing her the tea. "It's why I had to go back to my village."

"It is?" she asked, holding the warm cup between her hands.

"Yes. After I calmed down, I came back late at night to find you sleeping. I wasn't here but a minute before you began to have another nightmare."

"Oh," Eira whispered, staring down at the hot contents, drifting away in her thoughts. Truth was, she didn't know exactly why he had left her, but she had definitely not expected that. However, it was the fact that he could have touched her while she slept to form their bond but didn't that held her thoughts. Not once had he dared touch her as he watched her sleep, even once before his vow, and that said a lot about the reverent man before her.

Seeing her hesitation to begin drinking, he carefully sat down on the edge of the bed next to her and lightly cupped her scarred cheek. "Drink it, darling. Something tells me you have enough nightmares of your own."

Silently, she nodded, knowing he was right. She then raised the cup to let the tea pass her lips. Whatever he had put in it hadn't changed the taste of her grandmother's concoction, making her disbelieve it would do much of anything.

"So, as long as I drink that, I won't dream dreams that aren't mine anymore?"

"That's what Itako said, a seeress from my village," he clarified so she would understand. "Trust me; it will work," he assured her when she still didn't seem convinced.

The sight of Ryu turning into a dragon suddenly popped into her head, making her feel silly to think otherwise. *Oh, it'll work, all right.*

Taking another sip, she peeked through the open door, wanting to make sure her grandparents were still in the kitchen, drinking their nightly tea. Even though they were, she kept her voice to a whisper.

"You won't leave my side till I fall asleep, will you?"

"No, I won't," he promised with a smile, cupping her cheek again.

Eira started to relax and molded into his comforting touch. When their skin met, it was unlike anything she'd ever felt, and she could only describe it as an all-consuming fire scorching across every inch of her skin, and not until his touch met hers was the fire able to smother in a caressed, melting, icy touch.

At their first touch, the fire wasn't but a kindling, but by the time they had made it down the mountain to her house, they couldn't part, always needing to keep skin contact from the yearning burning inside. She remembered her grandmother's face when they had come in as her jaw had dropped to the floor in complete shock that she could be touched.

Her cheeks had blazed in embarrassment from them seeing her touch a boy for the first time, causing her to drop her hand from his and the flames to burn brighter through the evening. But now that they were alone again and able to touch, it calmed the fire inside.

Well ... slightly.

Desperately, she asked, "Is it always going to be like this?"

Ryu shook his head. "When we have fully mated, the feeling will dull. It'll only return this strong again if we don't touch for a while."

"So, we won't be able to ever leave each other?" The thought of that possibility made her happy inside.

Ryu thought for a moment, clearly thinking deeply through memories. "I never saw my parents too far away from each other growing up, so no, I don't think so."

Eira looked at him through heavy lashes, sensing something. "And now?"

"My mother is no longer with us."

Her stomach dropped at his words. "I'm so sorry, Ryu," she said, taking a hand from her warm cup to place over his.

"It's okay. I was a child when she passed, so it's been many years."

She noted that it didn't matter how many years ago it had been, time still didn't diminish the sadness in his voice when he spoke about his loss.

Suddenly needing to fix her dry throat, she swallowed while she thought about his other parent. "Your father ... he doesn't still *feel this*, does he?"

Solemnly, he shook his head. "No, I don't think so. I believe that part in him died along with her."

Again, the pain in his voice almost killed her, and as small of a relief as it was, it still was a relief to find out his father didn't feel the burn of the yearning touch, as that would have been simply cruel. She'd hate if something happened to her and Ryu was left like this. She felt bad enough as it was that she hadn't let him touch her, and he'd been like this for only days without her knowing.

"So"—she gulped, already almost knowing—"how do we *fully* mate?"

"Well, darling"—Ryu smiled seductively, letting her know it was exactly what she thought and that he appreciated the change in subject—"I don't think you're ready for that yet. Let's get you to your new home first."

Even with almost fully deaf grandparents, there certainly wasn't anything of that that could go on here, even if she were ready. But she wasn't, no matter how much it burned. It wasn't totally unbearable, *yet* ...

"This *is* my home," she whispered, knowing it was his duty to go back home, but she couldn't. She wasn't ready for that yet, either.

He contemplated for a few moments. "Would it make it easier if they gave you their blessing?"

"I'm not sure," she answered honestly, truly not knowing. With each passing second, it seemed like their bond grew stronger, so how could she not go with him either?

"Eira, they can't come. They aren't from my village." He told her the harsh reality, but then his voice softened. "Our magic won't allow it."

"How am I—" A frustrated Eira broke off, crying.

"Let's not worry about it tonight," he said, wiping away the tears that had fallen. "Let's worry about it tomorrow."

Sniffling, she nodded before taking the last sip of her tea then lay back in her bed, feeling the sudden exhaustion hit her.

Ryu was right; that could be tomorrow's freaking problem.

Wiping the last tear off her cheek as she started to drift to sleep, Ryu knew she was simply tired and overwhelmed by the day. She had, after all, found out his dragon-sized secret, witnessed him killing—*or should I say eating*—Kenshi, and that they were fated mates all in a single day.

And if that wasn't enough, the hormones being unlocked, coursing through her body, was surely enough.

His father had warned him when he'd find his fated mate, there would be a *significant* feeling of lust upon his first look, and for her, her first touch. He remembered his father telling him it was best to fully mate as soon as possible before the pain and hormones could kick in.

Unfortunately, it didn't matter how much his father had prepared him, because nothing could have prepared him for his fated mate. Eira had turned everything they knew about being mated upside down, and he wouldn't have it any other way.

Ryu let his thumb hum over the markings on her skin as if they were the most precious words ever written in braille.

There was only one thing left he needed to do before

they left for home, and it was time to find out what had caused Eira's own nightmares.

17

HOW SHE GOT HER SCARS

When he walked into the kitchen, Eira's grandparents were quietly finishing up their teas.

Upon meeting her grandmother, Ryu had become fond of the old bat. He couldn't help but think he was growing soft, as it was the second old lady he had grown a soft spot for. The love she held in her eyes for her granddaughter told him she would do anything possible for Eira. As for the grandfather, he didn't talk much, so as far as in-laws could go, there wasn't much not to like about them.

"Would you like a cup?" her grandmother asked, already getting up to do so.

Knowing he wouldn't want to offend the offer, as the lady obviously loved doting over people, he welcomed the hot drink. "That would be nice, thank you."

She took a small teacup from the shabby cabinet before pouring the still piping-hot tea into the cup then handed it to him.

Practically sensing he hadn't come in just for tea, she

sat back down in front of him and got right to it. "Is there something you need, Ryu?"

"Yes, actually." He cleared his throat, unbelieving he himself could get nervous. He never thought it possible, and when the second clearing of his throat didn't help much, he quickly took a sip before getting to the topic. "I would like to take Eira to my village to meet my father and …" He drawled out his next words. "I know it's soon, but if she likes it there and is happy, I'd like to ask her to marry me."

"Finally!" Her grandfather practically jumped up from where he sat; it was the quickest Ryu had seen the old man move since he'd met him. His withered hands had went up in the air in thanks. "You have my blessing, son. Whelp, good night."

Ryu almost couldn't believe what he had witnessed while watching the man, apparently riddled with arthritis, shimmy toward the kitchen door. It seemed like his job as a grandfather was finally done. It reminded him of his own father trying to mate him off; they acted as if it was the hardest job in the world.

The grandmother simply shook her head at her excited husband.

While it was great that he had Eira's grandfather's blessing, he wanted her grandmother's all the same, if not more after that show.

"I hope to have your blessing, too…"

Sitting back in her chair, she stared him down for a few moments, and then she finally smiled. "You do, and not just because *I want to get rid of her.*" She huffed toward where her husband left before she softened. "But the truth is, I'm going to miss her 'cause I'll only have … well, *that*, when she's gone."

He wanted to tell her sorry, because he couldn't stand the thought of his only company being the grandfather either, but he refrained himself.

Her grandmother drummed her fingers as she studied him suspiciously. She clearly sensed something else before voicing it. "Is there something else?"

"There is." He cleared his throat again, wondering why clairvoyance only came in the form of old witches. "I was actually hoping you could tell me what happened to Eira."

"You mean, how she got her scars," she clarified, being more specific.

Ryu nodded, taking another sip. "Yes."

Her drumming suddenly stopped. "And she didn't want to tell you?"

"Truthfully, I didn't ask," he answered, setting the cup back down on the table. "I was afraid she'd either omit or glaze over important details, and I want to hear ... *everything*."

"You're right; Eira would have," she simply agreed, confirming his fears. Taking one last drink, she finished her cup. "Give me a moment."

He watched her grandmother leave, and it took several minutes before she returned, and when she did, it was with a somber tone and a small box that she seemed to have kept for a few years.

As he stared down at the box now placed before him, his stomach dropped, feeling the impending doom of knowing the contents inside couldn't hold anything good.

It wasn't until her grandmother gave him the go-ahead, saying, "Go on," that he had the strength to do so.

When he removed the top, the first thing he saw was a framed photo. He recognized the little girl in the middle being Eira, but much younger. It was almost *strange* to see her without her scars from her burn; he had grown used to them, as it was one of the first things he had loved about her. But it was the smile she had not only on her lips but in her eyes that had him choking back emotion. He had yet to see her smile like that, and he made a vow right then and there to see it again. She looked so happy and content flanked between both parents, and it was clear that he was talking to Eira's grandmother on her paternal side.

"My son, Sato, got my wits and not so much his father's fishing abilities, so he left as soon as he could. He went to school on the other side of the world, and that's where he met Lysandra," she said with a reminiscing smile.

It was clear she didn't think their son had taken after his father, but looking down at the photo, Ryu thought he was the spitting image of him. When his eyes moved to Lysandra, he understood where Eira had gotten her beauty. With matching porcelain skin and ruby hair, she mostly took after her mother with few attributes from her father, but it was enough to know she also belonged on this side of the earth. It was what made Eira more alluring than her own mother, and that was saying something.

Setting the framed photo to the side, the next thing he saw was a black and white newspaper clipping. He had never actually seen one in real life, but he had seen enough of them in his world studies to know what it was.

The same photo he had held in his hands was plastered on the front page of the thin newspaper, and what was once a colorful photo of a beautiful family now seemed ominous in a grainy black and white version. The words that followed were just as haunting ...

FAMILY ATTACKED BY FIRE

A family enjoying a Sunday stroll through the city that turned horrific when they were attacked by one lone man with a tank of gasoline and a lighter. Their attacker quickly doused the father, Sato Sho, from head to toe before setting him ablaze. The mother, Lysandra Sho, and daughter, Eira Sho, were taken to the hospital for their own injuries due to the proximity of the backsplash. The mother later died, and the daughter remains in critical condition. Attacker, Arthur Abrahms, remains in county jail and awaits sentencing.

The horrendous image Ryu held in his mind would only grow more detailed as he read through the following police reports and accounts from witnesses. Tears that would dare to spill, he kept in with an iron strength, letting them only fuel the fire inside with each word he read as he finally went through Eira's own heart-wrenching account.

When he set the last page down in disgust, the grandmother showed her own.

"We were all she had left after that." Her voice then changed to a whisper. "That's how Eira ended up all the way here."

Trying to wet his throat, Ryu gripped the teacup, only to send the cooled contents to boil again before it quickly burst.

"I'm sorry," he exasperated after her small shrill, knocking some sense into him to calm himself.

"I-It's quite all right," she said, shaking her head in disbelief.

He could see she wanted to question what she had just seen but didn't dare to ask in fear he would think she was crazy to think his tea had boiled over, which had caused it to burst.

Picking up the broken pieces, he tried to play it off. "Sometimes, I don't know my own strength."

"I see that." She laughed, going to help clean up the mess, but he wouldn't let her.

"I got it," Ryu assured her, not wanting her to get burned by the liquid and to feel how hot it had gotten. It was already a small miracle none had splashed on her, and another one that she had let him do it himself.

As he wiped off the liquid that had splashed on the papers before placing everything back in the box, her grandmother continued, "I only got the reports because I told them it might be useful to a therapist over here when she was ready to talk, and they agreed. I could never get her to go talk to one, but I knew she'd need someone to understand what she went through, so I made that box in hopes one day it would."

Ryu closed the box, solemnly nodding understanding, but there was still one thing he didn't understand. "Why is she so afraid to be touched?"

Grandmother's eyes turned fearsome, clearly remembering something horrid. "May you never have to walk through a burn victim unit and hear their screams, Ryu. I wouldn't wish it upon a single soul. Even if I didn't still hear her screams from her nightmares, I could never forget the sound of her screams every time they changed her bandages *for a year* in the hospital. All the poking and prodding along with it, to such a young girl after what she had horrifically gone through and lost, is something I'll never understand how she survived mentally. I know I couldn't."

With his anger rising again, he understood everything clearly now. Whether Eira ever decided to tell him none of it, some of it, or all of it one day, he knew all he needed to know.

Well, *almost*.

Seeing a shard he had missed, he picked up the sharp piece, needing to know one last thing. "And where is Arthur now?"

18

HORRIFICALLY FATEFUL DAY

Every Sunday after lunch, Eira and her parents walked the city. It was their little family ritual that they had started, and they'd always stop in a shop they hadn't gone to before for a little sweet treat before they'd turn back around.

She couldn't tell you how their ritual had begun in the first place, only that Sunday was their favorite day, and they looked forward to it all week.

"See anything that looks good, ladies?" her father asked them when they had journeyed as far as they had gone before.

Her mother, Lysandra, only smiled at her daughter to see what she thought. "Eira?"

A young Eira looked around at all the shops, but they all looked quite familiar. "I think we've been to them all."

"I think you're quite right, honey," her father, Sato, agreed. "A bit farther, then."

Eira could sense the bit of hesitation in her mother, but she reluctantly agreed with her husband to go a bit farther.

They walked only a few streets over, trying to find a good-looking shop filled with treats to Eira's liking, when it became obvious they might have strayed too far.

"I think we should go back now," Sato mentioned when they witnessed a man lighting a trash can on fire.

"Yes." Lysandra quickly nodded in agreement when the man caught sight of them and gave them a distasteful look. It was obvious the man didn't approve of the different-looking family, so she held on to her daughter's hand tighter as they turned back around.

Getting the idea she should be fearful, Eira noticed a different man on the sidewalk who was covered in a dirty blanket. She had only passed him moments ago and didn't think anything of him, but now she saw her surroundings in a different light since she was no longer concerned about looking in the different shops.

When she stepped closer to her mother to avoid him, the action made her mother, who was between them, move closer to her husband.

Time seemed to slow when the man with the gasoline tank must've rushed up behind them to cut them off. Not knowing exactly what he would do, it was certain the last thing any of them ever expected was for him to pour the contents of the tank all over her father, and then it was simply too late.

With them being so close together, a lot of the gasoline also splashed on Lysandra, and some of it splashed on Eira's face, along with the hand that held her mother's.

The flash of a lighter that flipped to life before it was thrown onto her father felt like time moving so slowly, and yet there was simply nothing you could do about it. When you were already dunked in fluid, there was nothing to do except kill yourself faster.

That vile man only held their life in his hands for a single *moment before he tossed them away no differently than the pile of trash in a can.*

All Eira could do was scream in horror as she watched her father burn in a fiery blaze before she watched her mother, and then finally herself. Her horrific screams were not only from the physical pain but the pain of watching her parents die, and it was all she could do before a blanket was cocooned around her.

She would later come to find out that it had been the home-less man who had thrown his only blanket over her, and by the time he could put out Eira's fire and do the same for her mother, it would be too late—the burns had covered too much of Mom's body while it was rendered completely useless to even try the life-saving method on her father.

At only fourteen, she would never forget the smell of gasoline right before the smell of not only her own burning flesh but her dying parents'. And, for the next year, Eira would often sit in her hospital bed, wondering who got the worst fate of them all ...

Was it her father, who had died after a few agonizing minutes but eventually felt the sweet relief of death? Or her mother, who wouldn't die until hours later at the hospital? Or was it her, who would undergo so many treatments just to be scarred for life anyway, along with the constant memory of that horrifically fateful day.

19

DON'T MOVE

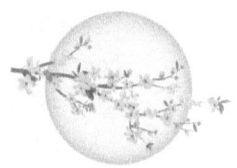

"I think"—Eira forced a cough—"I'm still sick."

Looking at her suspiciously, he sat down next to her on the bed. "Really?"

"Mmhmm." She touched her forehead, hoping he'd buy it. "I'm still running a fever."

He called her bluff by removing her hand to place his on her forehead then tried to feel for warmth. "You don't feel warm."

"Oh, what do you know?" Eira huffed, shooing his hand away, "You're a dragon, for goodness' sake; how are you supposed to *feel* if I'm running a fever, anyway?"

"Is this about leaving?" Seeing that it clearly was, he continued, "Eira, I—" only to suddenly stop when her grandmother came barreling in.

"What's wrong?"

Eira tried her best to up her acting game and managed a sniffle. "I think I'm still sick."

Carefully looking her granddaughter over, she let out a sigh. "Ryu, why don't you give us a moment?"

Giving her hand a light squeeze, he then got up and left

the room. They both felt the sudden loss and the slight burn intensify as he left.

Oh, shut up, she told her screaming body, having to remind herself that Ryu was a traitor for not believing she was sick in the first place.

Taking his place on the bed beside her, Grandmother seemed strangely demure today. "Honey, I don't think you are still sick. I think this is about something else."

Eira sat quietly, not saying anything.

"It's time for you to go live your life now, honey."

What? The pit in her stomach made her want to throw up. She couldn't believe she had heard her right, but her grandmother's face told her she had. How could she leave her frail and old grandparents now?

"But—"

"We will manage," she assured her with a loving smile, knowing exactly what she was going to say. "We've lived our lives, and now it's time for you to go live yours."

Defeated, Eira's shoulders slumped. She only hoped Ryu wouldn't hear her confession on the other side of the door as she whispered, "I'm scared."

"Oh, Eira. Do you know how I know you'll be fine?" she asked with tears welling in her proud eyes.

Eira simply shook her head and, for the first time, her grandmother didn't retract her touch when her withered hands cupped her scarred cheek to remind her of something important.

"Because you are the bravest person I know."

And for another first time, Eira didn't pull away either. Instead, she leaned into it, welcoming the touch as they both cried like babies they had claimed her not to be anymore. The beautiful moment didn't get ruined until her grandfather walked in.

"Can I help you pack?"

"Ryu, I need to be packing," she said, stomping up behind him on the small trail.

"You don't want to go back to the place we met?"

"I mean, yes, of course, I do, but I also don't want to leave my grandparents to do all the work packing ..." *Who was she kidding?* "I mean, my grandmother."

"She was the one who suggested we go for a walk, remember?"

"Right." She shook her head. The pressure of everything hitting her at once was making her crazy.

"So, relax," he told her cooly, taking her hand as they got closer to the edge. They both sat down on her favorite spot where he had caught her sleeping.

Looking out at the little island, she couldn't believe that was her future home, and also that it was even inhabitable in the first place. Shutting her eyes, she fell back onto the earth then opened them to look up at the big blue sky. "I'm going to miss this."

"I know," he whispered back, lying down with her. "I promise I think you'll like your new home." Turning his head to look at her, he was even sincere when he said, "And if you don't, then you can come back."

Eira laughed, sensing how painful that had to be to say, but it truly made her feel better. "Thanks."

Letting go of her hand, he moved her chin to look at him so his lips could capture hers in a searing kiss, and when they parted, she could feel the slight stinging.

This time *she* kissed *him* to take the pain away, and it took only a second before lust consumed her.

Ryu pushed into her body, feeling his own need and deepening the kiss. She could feel just how heavy he was, yet he still restrained himself by not giving her his full weight. His mouth traveled to the scars on her cheeks, kissing them tenderly before his lips finally went down her neck.

"Oh my ..." she hotly whispered in a steamy haze.

Taking back her mouth and silencing her before she could think too much, he held her hips in a tight grip as he spun them to his back with her on top of him.

Her eyes grew wide at his brazenness, and then she was suddenly aware of the power she held to be above a dragon. In control, she took her own liberties, kissing him like he had her. She kissed down his neck, and, feeling a rush of bravery, she sucked on the tender flesh.

"I'd stop before you go too far, darling."

Eira immediately did at his rough tone.

Sensing the sudden power shift, and the hardness under her hips, she realized she never actually held any power at all over Ryu and that he was simply letting her feel like she was.

"Sorry," she said, rolling off him before she got more than she bargained for. Eira wanted nothing more than to give in to her needs, but that was her body full of mating hormones talking, not her. She wanted her own mind to be certain that she wanted Ryu wholeheartedly.

"It's all right," he assured her, still trying to get himself under control. "You can only tempt the dragon so far." After taking a few moments for himself, he finally stood and held out his hand to help her up. "You ready?"

Eira looked confused. "For what?"

"To go home."

"Sure," she said with a bittersweet smile, knowing it was probably their last time here, but she needed to get back to helping her grandmother pack.

"I have a surprise for you first, though."

"You do?" she asked, intrigued.

"Yes, I just need you to stand right here." He moved her quite a bit from the edge, placing her right where he wanted her. "Now close your eyes ... and no matter what, *don't move.*"

Laughing through dark lids in excitement, she seemed to miss the seriousness in his tone at that last request. "Why?"

"Don't worry about it. Just promise me you won't move, all right?"

She swore, finally catching on that she really shouldn't move. "Fine, I promise."

"Good. Now wait here and keep your eyes closed."

And Eira did just that, knowing he'd give her hell if she peeked, but she really couldn't help it when the wind picked up and started rushing over her face. What harm could one little peek do?

Trying to peek through slitted eyes was when she saw it —the dragon-sized version of Ryu rushing right toward her. I mean, he had told her not to move and, truthfully, as much as she wanted to run, she couldn't. Becoming completely immobile in fear kept her frozen like a scared statue.

One second, her feet were firmly on the ground and in another, they were high in the sky. Again, she found herself flying in the clutches of the dragon.

"Ryu!" she screamed out, hoping he could somehow hear her.

Mocking laughter rang in her head. *Yes, darling?*

"Put me—"

No need to scream. I can hear you just fine.

"—down!" she continued anyway, hoping he'd get her message.

I will once we get home.

Eira managed to open her eyes back up, seeing her adored cliff get smaller and smaller. "You're going the wrong way!"

No, I'm not, his dragon whispers assured her.

She should've known he'd pull a stunt like this.

"But what about my stuff? I didn't finish packing."

You don't need anything where we're going.

"But my grandmother, she's still packing—"

She's not, he assured her.

"How do you know?" She was rather tempted to hit him if it wouldn't cause her to fall to her death.

The dragon simply laughed. *Why do you think she said to go for a walk?*

"It was her idea?" Eira screamed, again in shock.

Well, she didn't know we'd be flying to get there, but I told her I could be convincing enough to get you to keep walking to my home.

She almost couldn't believe it, and flying through the sky in the clutches of a dragon wasn't what she couldn't believe. It was the fact that they'd do something like that to her.

But then Ryu told her what her own heart knew to be true.

We both knew you would never go if you weren't tricked into leaving, Eira.

20

WELCOME TO KASUMI ISLAND

Once Eira's feet had safely touched the ground, the pit in her stomach eased.

"I can't believe you did that." As soon as he started to shift, she began to lay into him. "Take me back home—"

"Ahem." Ryu tried to interrupt her, but Eira continued on, still not noticing.

"Right now, Ryu!"

"Eira …" he grumbled out a whisper, but it was his synthetic smile he was putting on that made Eira finally take notice.

Oh no. Immediately, that pit in her stomach returned upon seeing the crowd of villagers that surrounded them. Her earlier need to touch the ground had kept her from noticing their audience in the first place. Of course, the villagers of the island could see Ryu in his dragon form unlike the rest of the world, so they had witnessed their arrival. It made it clear to Eira that she had a lot to learn.

"Just smile," he whispered over to her again, taking her hand in his as they started walking. Giving her strength, he gave her hand a squeeze. "Welcome to Kasumi Island."

Feeling self-conscious for a girl like Eira was a severe understatement for how she felt in this moment. Especially considering how beautiful the women not only *were* but in what they *wore*— beautiful, embroidered silks of all different lustrous colors. It wouldn't have mattered if Eira knew she was coming and had picked her nicest outfit— nothing would have been nice enough to come here. It was no wonder Ryu had said she didn't need to bring anything —not a single thing she had belonged here, not even her ...

Holding on to his hand for strength, she prayed for this to be over quickly as they continued walking. And as they passed the people, her mouth began to drop when each one bowed. At first, she thought it was only to him, but then she got an eerie tingling feeling on the back of her neck that it was also for her. Hearing the whispers of "queen" whispered throughout the crowd solidified those feelings.

Afraid she was about to pass out from the attention, Eira dragged her feet slower, thinking she'd rather go back to flying the skies in the clutch of a dragon than this.

"Ryu ..."

"You're okay. I'm right here," he quietly assured her that she could do this. "And I know you will not *disappoint* me."

Strangely, at his words, the last thing she wanted to do was disappoint Ryu.

Since the incident, Eira had always felt like a disappointment not only in life but to everyone and everything, including her dead parents. In this moment, she might have been less than adequate on the outside, but she'd be damned if she was less than adequate for her fated mate on the inside, too. So, even though Eira didn't quite know where the sudden spirit came from, she continued on, hoping to prove not only to him *but to herself* that she could do it.

Holding her head high to the best of her abilities, she thought she would be grateful to reach his home, but she suddenly came upon seeing what she could only describe as palace doors. Swallowing hard, she only hoped what awaited inside would be a lot easier to take.

I mean, this has to be the worst of it, right?

When they entered the safety of the palace, she was happy to find it desolate. She was about to tell him how hard what she had just done was for her, but her thoughts were taken away by the beauty of the architecture and the intricately ornate things around that were either the color of Ryu's dragon or made of jade.

"Wow ..." Eira breathed, her breath taken away.

"Do you like it?" he asked, staring at her like how she did the beauty of her surroundings.

Too wrapped up in looking at everything around her, she missed the pride on Ryu's face for what she had just done.

"Do I like it?" she scoffed, wondering who possibly couldn't. "It's the most beautiful thing I've ever seen."

"It took me a while to get used to it as well."

Eira hadn't even heard anyone entering; she turned to find an older man and a young woman standing directly behind her. If they had been a snake, they could have bitten her.

Both of them bowed their heads as Ryu introduced them.

"This is my sensei, Kage, and his daughter, Yuri," he said before proudly waving his hand toward her. "And this is Eira ... my fated mate."

Blushing from the shock of him introducing her that

way, Eira politely bowed back with a kind smile. "Hello."

"We are honored to meet you and serve you in any way we can," Kage announced before placing a firm hand on Ryu's shoulder. "I've been training you since you were a little boy, and I couldn't be happier for you. You have waited a long time for this, Ryu—we all have."

Yuri smiled sweetly at Ryu. "We both couldn't be happier."

At her smile, Eira felt like a dull caterpillar next to an alluring butterfly. Yuri made the villagers outside look less than in comparison, and Eira had already thought herself inadequate enough next to them.

She hated comparing herself to other girls, but Eira found she couldn't help it as she stood next to Yuri, who was flawless perfection. Lowering her sleeves out of habit to cover more of the scars on her hand, she let her veil of fiery locks do the same to her face. She only hoped Ryu wouldn't take notice of her sudden lack of already barely-there confidence.

"Is Father here?" Ryu asked.

"In the other room, I believe." Kage motioned with his head in the correct direction. "I hope to see you tomorrow, bright and early. You haven't trained in a while, and I expect to get you back in shape."

Ryu simply laughed and said from over his shoulder, "Yeah, you wish."

"Nice to meet you both," Eira quickly said before they disappeared.

Not finding his father where he had expected him, Ryu decided for them to stay put. "I'm sure he will be here any minute."

Her nerves only somehow seemed to skyrocket knowing she was going to meet his father, but truly, the palace was such a work of art that it kept her distracted for another moment. Her eyes landed on a smoky black vase that had golden veins branching out like lightning that reminded her of the scars on her body.

Noticing her fondness for the piece, Ryu smiled, clearly remembering a fond memory. "My mother picked that vase."

Her fingertips carefully ran along one of the golden veins. "Well, she has good taste."

"That she did," a strong voice echoed across the walls. "I see you have returned and, this time, with what you should have brought with you last time."

"I have," Ryu forced out with a squared jaw, bowing to his father with what seemed like difficulty. Then he introduced her, "This is Eira, my fated mate."

She tried her best not to blush again, though she really didn't think she'd ever get used to him introducing her that way. It made her heart sing that he would introduce her with such pride.

"Eira," he continued the formalities, "this is my father, Tatsu."

"Well, Eira ..." his father drawled out, giving her a once-over, "nice to *finally* meet you."

Eira bowed to him as low as she could, hoping to hide her nervous expression, but she was certain her voice gave her nerves away. "Lovely to meet you, too."

He gave her hand in his a squeeze; it was as if Eira could understand so much in just a touch, and she was grateful.

"So ..." Ryu seemed to take on nerves of his own. "Did it happen in time?"

Tatsu looked at the hands intertwined between them, noticing something that Eira would soon find out later. "Go look for yourself."

21

A FRIEND

Eira stared up at the impressive but barren tree. She could only imagine what it must've been like full and in its prime.

"Did he tell you about it?"

Looking over at the man who had just joined her peacefully on the bench, she nodded. "He did."

Ryu had told her everything about it, all the way from the tether between them to how the cycle restarted with each new heir ...

Dropping her hand when they reached the sight of the tree, Ryu seemed heartbroken.

"I was too late."

She watched the tears form in his eyes with his shattered emotions. She had never seen him like this, and there was nothing she could do or say for him in that moment because she simply didn't understand what he was talking about nor the importance of the tree.

Moving toward the mythical beast, Ryu placed his hand on

the trunk and dropped hard to his knees. "How ...? What ...?" he began to croak out in disbelief.

Eira wasn't sure, but the tears that streamed down his face now seemed ... happy?

Quickly, Ryu shot up to his feet, looking up at the bare branches as if he were searching for something.

He disappeared from her sight at the vastness of the base of the tree as he went around, and it wasn't until she heard him say, "Eira, come here," that she followed him around and found him staring up toward the top of the tree. "Do you see it?"

Trying her best to line her eyes up with his line of sight, she was about to give up until she finally saw it. A perfectly pink cherry blossom petal that lightly swayed in the wind.

And that was when he began.

"One day, new life will blossom this tree again, and you'll see it filled with a million of them ..."

All that she had learned had been a lot for her to take in, so she had asked for a moment alone.

The pressure that was now placed on her shoulders had instantly weighed her down, and she knew instinctively that her fated mate's father wasn't about to make it any better.

"The tree's leaves had only half-fallen when I met my Kana."

She could hear so much in that sentence—pride and loss for his wife mainly, but there was something else hidden in his words that she didn't quite understand yet. However, she was almost certain he would enlighten her.

"I'm sorry to hear about her," was simply all she could think to say before he continued.

"I remember sitting right here with him when the first one fell when he was only seven. He has waited many years to find you, Eira. And you must know that things like *time* are very different for us."

Eira listened intently, knowing he was about to reveal something Ryu had ceased to mention.

"To be born with the magic of the dragon means time moves differently for us." Seeing she was quickly catching on, he told her before she could ask, "Ryu is much older than you probably think him to be."

Her eyes grew wide in shock. "Really?"

"He has lived three of your lifetimes already," he confirmed.

"*Three?*" she whispered in disbelief.

"It was one of the reasons why I kept him here on the island so long before I let him leave in search for you—I simply thought his fated mate hadn't been born yet." Taking in her look of age, he didn't want to sell himself short. "Turns out I wasn't *necessarily* wrong."

Now her head practically spun with questions, but Tatsu seemed to know the first one that came to mind.

"Our magic is definitely a wonder, but you need not to worry; our fated mates are born with a little magic themselves that only activates when you meet. So, your aging clock will now slow with Ryu's."

Some bit of relief flooded her. "That's good to know."

"However," he began again, his tone slightly harsh, "the magic you hold is very dull, so what *you feel* is *very little* compared to what the dragon inside of him lets him feel."

Eira wasn't understanding the point he was trying to make ...until she did.

"For instance, the pain you feel by not completing the mating dance is simply *pitiful* in comparison." His words started to lash against her. "The pain you are causing him, Eira, is cruel."

"I ...I ...I ..." Her mind had gone blank, and her mouth didn't know what response it should give, either. It was true; she did feel pain, but to know she was causing Ryu an insurmountable amount cut her to the quick.

Glossy tears coated her eyes, daring to fall. Truthfully, in that moment, she was close to running away but only stayed put when they gained an audience.

"My King." Yuri bowed lowly. "I'd love to show Eira to her room."

"That would be nice, thank you, Yuri. I'm sure Eira will have much to learn from you."

The way Tatsu looked at Yuri warmly, with kindness in his eyes, was how she hoped her fated mate's father would look at her but, pulling down her sleeves to cover her burns, she knew that was never, *ever* going to happen.

"Thank you for your ... *knowledge*," Eira said, struggling to find the right word before gratefully leaving. She had hoped her eyes wouldn't dare spill the salty liquid, and she was thankful when they hadn't.

However, there was certainly no fooling the girl.

"Don't worry," Yuri tried her best to comfort her. "He was quite intimidating the first few years I was around him."

"I don't know if that's a good thing." Eira laughed through fallen tears now, instantly feeling comfortable around the sweet woman. She supposed she should be happy that Tatsu had even treated Yuri coldly at first. Then again, having to take years to warm to a person seemed a bit much.

"It will get better, I promise," Yuri assured her quietly as they walked through the palace. "I am your lady in waiting, so feel free to call upon me for anything you might need."

"My lady in waiting?" she asked, not understanding.

Yuri smiled, reiterating for her, "Just consider me your personal helper."

Oh my, Eira thought, nodding in understanding. Tatsu was right ... there was quite a lot she needed to learn.

When they reached two huge doors, Yuri pushed them open. "This is your room."

Eira's jaw practically hit the floor. "M-my room?"

"Of course." She laughed at her like she was silly and waved for her to go inside. "Hopefully, it is to your liking."

"Yeah." She desperately swallowed, trying to wet her dry throat. "You could say that."

Thankfully, her sarcastic tone hadn't gone over Yuri's head. "I'm sure it's a lot for you to take in."

Eira nodded and finally entered, realizing she could put her grandparents' whole house into just this room. The sheer size of it was what had taken her by surprise at first, but now that she looked around, it was the things inside, like the luxurious bedding that had her even more overwhelmed by the difference in how she and Ryu had lived.

Yuri went to the closet door and threw them open to reveal it was large in size as well, and stuffed full. "Would you like to pick something to wear for dinner, or shall I?"

Eira entered the closet, speechless, touching the lush fabrics, her belly fluttering. "Whose things are these?"

"Yours," Yuri said simply. "I'm sure some things may have belonged to Ryu's mother, but I'd say, considering how sentimental Tatsu is over his late wife's things, most of it are items Ryu has chosen over the years."

Again, Eira lacked the words for not only a response but for how she felt. Everything in here was beautiful and didn't lack for taste.

Overwhelmed by choice, she finally got her tongue and

mind to work in unison. "It might be best for you to choose. I'm not quite sure what would be best."

"Certainly," Yuri agreed with a twinkle in her eyes.

Eira could only imagine the girl had waited for this moment to finally look through the many beautiful things that had been collected. She could tell her lady in waiting had impeccable taste as well, with not only what she chose for Eira to wear but in how put together she herself looked.

When she was fully dressed, she was thankful Yuri had chosen something demure in comparison to the flashy things she had seen the women wear outside of the palace. She was used to wearing dark colors so as not to stand out, and she really was happy that Yuri seemed to understand her so well already. Even when she had helped brush her hair, Yuri had pulled her hair back off her face, but once she saw how uncomfortable Eira looked, she let the silky red strands go without so much of a word needing to be said.

"Now it's time for my favorite part," Yuri continued on, making her feel comfortable. "Jewelry."

Both looked over the many different and ornate options when Yuri landed on a beautiful pearl ring. "This is stunning."

"It is," Eira agreed, seeing the twinkle brighten in her eyes.

She held the ring out for Eira to take. "This will match perfectly."

Smiling, Eira closed Yuri's hand over it. "For your kindness."

Yuri violently shook her head. "Oh, I couldn't possibly."

"You can, and you will." She let her know she wouldn't take no for an answer. "Besides, I have so much that Ryu will never know."

"Thank you," Yuri finally gave in, putting it in her

pocket before grabbing a dainty necklace that Eira thought was much more suited to her.

"Now, that is perfect." Eira beamed, seeing that she was being so easily understood.

Grateful someone here besides Ryu was nice to her, and that she had a confidant, it finally felt like, for once, Eira had actually made a friend.

22

IS THAT A DEAL?

"He hates me." Eira helplessly slumped down on the bed once they were in the confines of her new room.

"Who?" Ryu asked, raising a brow. "My father?"

"Yes," she breathed like it was obvious.

"No, he doesn't." He approached to comfort her, then placed his arm over her shoulders and let her know why his father had perhaps been the least welcoming. "He is disappointed in me for almost costing us the dynasty."

"Well, you're his son, so he'll get over it." She tossed his arm off her shoulder and got back to her feet, unable to keep from pacing. "Look at me, though. I'm simply ... inadequate."

"Eira, don't say that about yoursel—"

"It's true. Look at me." She gestured at herself, trying to send her point home, but Ryu simply wasn't having it.

"Enough." This time, his tone came out rather harshly; he didn't appreciate her manner of speaking about herself. "I don't want to ever hear you talk about yourself that way again. Do you understand me?"

She didn't know how or when he had gotten up and closed the distance between them, only that she now stood staring up at an enraged man who could change into a dragon at any second if it pleased him so.

"Do you understand?" he repeated when she had been too breathless to answer.

Managing a nod was the best she could do in this moment.

"Good," Ryu said once he was certain she wouldn't be making that mistake again. As he continued with his next critique, he let his voice soften. "Your choice in attire, however, leaves a lot to be desired."

Even though he tried his best to say it in a joking manner, she knew the truth held behind it, making her feel completely defeated now. "You don't like it?"

Seeing her hurt, he desperately tried to sound nicer but still had to be honest. "I'm not that fond of the color. I had something like that in mind for if you were mourning."

"*Mourning*?" She was appalled at how horrible he was with his words in this moment. He was quite literally being the opposite of comforting when she had just literally flown across the ocean to live in his home.

Sensing that he was making things worse, he quickly explained his thinking. "As royalty, it's best to wear them for such occasions."

"Oh ..." She licked her dry lips, remembering his mother's fate. "I see."

Ryu sighed. "Did you not like the things I bought?"

"What? Of course I did." She was taken off guard and now felt guilty, understanding why he had brought it up in the first place. She could now see the hurt in *his* eyes when she reached for his hand. "They are all lovely. Every single thing is extraordinary, and I thank you for all the thought and care you clearly put in picking each piece." She made sure he knew she was sincere because she was. Truthfully, she was. "But ... I just don't want all that attention, *at first*," Eira clarified before she could get his hopes up. "I need to get used to it, is all."

The corner of his lip lifted in a slow smile. "I understand. You need time."

"Thank you." Relief flooded her that she could hold on to the security of wearing darker colors a bit longer. His comment, however, brought her to the next point she had wanted to ask during dinner. "Ryu ... how old are you?"

Silence enveloped them for a few moments before he finally answered, "Old-*er*." At once, he knew by her face that she was clearly not only unimpressed by his particular wording, but he answered with a shrug, "Honestly, at my age, you kind of lose count."

"And you didn't think to tell me?" Frustration was evident in her voice.

"Time moves differently for me, so I'm *technically* your age, give or take a few years. Besides, it doesn't exactly change the fact I'm your fated mate, now does it?"

"No," she grumbled in defeat after several cursed thoughts. "But it would have been nice to know."

"I apologize for not telling you," he said sincerely.

"Is there anything else you'd like to tell me?"

"Well ..." It was obvious by his starting tone that there was. "You will age slower now, too."

"I know that already," Eira grumbled again, letting him know he was too late telling her that as well.

"Okay, well, good. That should be it, then," Ryu confirmed, like a weight had been lifted ... almost. "I *think*."

Eira couldn't help but laugh at him, knowing he wasn't capable of being malicious toward her. He was right; even if

Ryu had been alive since the dawn of time, nothing would matter with the pull they felt between each other.

Twisting his hand in hers, she was reminded of the longing that coursed through her body and the words his father had told her earlier.

The pain you are causing him, Eira, is cruel.

She noticed the flex in his jaw just by the simple action, which did let her know *it was true.*

For the first time, Eira was the one to initiate intimacy between them. Kissing him passionately, she pushed at his chest until he backed up to the bed. When she gave him a harder shove, he took the hint and fell back down on top of it.

With him now eye level with her, her fingertips slowly went to the buttons of her top.

Ryu was so captured by her beauty that it wasn't until she had released three of the small gold buttons and got an eyeful of the tops of her breasts that he noticed she was undressing. If he let her undo just one more button, he was certain they would splay free, and then he'd no longer be certain that he could stop her.

He grabbed her hands to cease her from going further, and his voice came out hoarse, making it sound much harsher than he had intended. "What are you doing?"

"What do you think I'm doing?" she asked, shooing his hands away in an attempt to continue.

"As much as I'd love to," Ryu grumbled painfully, capturing her hands in a loving but tighter grip, "I know you're not ready yet."

"I am." She tried her best to convince him, and when she wasn't sure it had worked, she swept his mouth up in a fervent kiss, hoping it would make him forget.

He kissed her back for only a moment before Ryu's wits

returned. Rising back to his feet, he put distance between them. "What's going on, Eira?"

"I-I-I thought this is what you wanted?" she asked, confused.

"It is, but not if you're not ready," he assured her gruffly before his tone turned sweet. "My only desire is to have you willing and wanting it as much as me."

Eira slumped down again, defeated. "Sorry."

"You do not need to apologize." He grabbed her face, rubbing his thumb over the burns on her cheek. "I just don't understand where this came from all of a sudden." He was just as confused.

"I-I just thought it was something I was supposed to do, is all." She decided to keep the reason why to herself.

"I would never ask you to do anything you do not *want* to do, Eira. I apologize if I made you think otherwise. I know moving here and changing your whole life are things I might have expected from you, but you do have free will, and I will no longer make you feel otherwise."

She knew he meant every word. The relief that flooded her brought her to tears. It hadn't even been a full day, and she hated it here, wanting nothing more than to go back home. And now, she didn't have to hide it.

"I don't think I belong here, Ryu," she whispered truthfully.

"Oh, Eira," he crooned, wiping up the fallen tear. Then, when she continued to sob uncontrollably, he held her close to his chest. "You would not be my fated mate if you didn't."

She tried to get her words out through the harsh sobs, but it took a moment, afraid he wouldn't actually let her. "Can ... I ... go ... back ... home?"

"You can." He nodded. "But could you give me just one

more day? And then, if you still want to leave, I'll fly you back home tomorrow night ... Is that a deal?"

Eira sniffled, already feeling lighter. "Deal." Flying in the clutches of his dragon form again didn't sound like fun, but she'd gladly do it to get back home.

Just one more day. She smiled before letting out a big yawn. Today had been long, and it was starting to catch up with her.

"I almost forgot." Ryu reached into his pocket for the small vial that was supposed to help her dreams. "One drop."

"P-Please, can I-I go?" she pleaded, fearing what her future might hold from this moment forward.

Lucca stared down at her, bringing his hand up close to her face. "I don't think you understand."

Chloe's breath caught in her throat. She desperately wanted to close her eyes, but his wouldn't let her, forcing her to remain looking up at him.

"There is no leaving," he continued, careful not to touch her, though he twirled a strand of her silky black hair around his finger. "You're mine now, Chloe."...

Eira suddenly awoke, grateful to not have woken up Ryu with her night terrors. She didn't know how he would have felt about her not taking her potion when she'd told him she had. Truthfully, she had no idea why she hadn't just taken it. All she had was a feeling that she was dreaming these dreams for a reason. But after that one, she no longer cared to find out the reasoning. The man named Lucca was simply too menacing.

Quickly adjusting her eyes to the darkness, she quietly took the vial sitting on the bedside table that was supposed to keep her dreams at bay and dropped a single drop to the tip of her finger before placing it on her tongue. Taking a deep breath, she put it back and got comfortable again, watching a peacefully sleeping Ryu with a content smile on her face.

Eira was able to go back to sleep with the thought she was certain that Ryu was nothing—*nothing*—like the man who had been haunting her dreams.

23

SENSEI RYU

"Can you tell me where we're going now?" she asked after they had left the palace doors. She was happy to get fresh air, though she still saw the man's strange eyes from her nightmare, but she quickly pushed it out of her mind, knowing today would be a good day, as she could go home tonight, if she pleased.

"No." Ryu laughed, sensing her eagerness. "It's a surprise."

"Fine," she grumbled, giving in. The excitement of what he was going to show her had been eating away at her since he'd told her to get dressed this morning. Looking over at Ryu, she noticed he still looked as tired as he had earlier, only now he seemed to walk a bit stiffly. "Are you all right?"

Ryu rubbed his shoulder a bit, trying to massage out a kink. "Yes, I trained with Kage while you slept early this morning, and I think he was right; I did get out of shape."

"We can go back and let you rest—"

"I'll be all right," he assured her, having no thoughts of turning back. "Besides, what we're about to do will loosen me up."

Eira knew that was his one and only hint about where they were going, and now she was worried about what she was wearing. "I'm not sure I'm dressed for an activity."

Ryu scanned at her long silk dress robe. "You're dressed fine."

She could tell he still didn't care for the color, but Eira had loved it the second Yuri had shown it to her.

As they passed by some villagers, one old man came up to her and bowed his head at them. "For you."

Eira looked at the beautiful red flower being held out to her. "Thank you." She smiled politely and accepted it. Spinning it between her fingertips, she took in the spikey, strange yet wonderful-looking petals. When she was about to lift it to her nose to smell it, Ryu took the precious gift from her before she could.

"Allow me." Sweeping the strands of hair that covered the left side of her face, he tucked them preciously behind her ear to reveal his scarred beauty in all her glory before placing the flower there to rest above her ear.

The red flower against her red hair showed the difference between fire and blood. Two red colors so similar yet so different.

Ryu bowed at the gentleman's kind gesture before he took her hand to continue their journey, which wasn't much farther at all.

When they came upon an empty, warm wooden building with large windows, it only made her more confused, as she didn't have any inclination what they might do. She took her shoes off, like Ryu did, and sat on the floor right where he told her to.

It wasn't until young children started flooding in and calling him "Sensei Ryu" that she knew *exactly* what was happening.

I'll be damned.

"What's so funny?" Ryu asked with a sly smile when he took his position.

"So, you really *do* teach martial arts to children."

Once Ryu clapped, she got her answer as each kid took their place and perfectly bowed.

"Everyone, this is Eira," he introduced her to the kids. "Give her a big hello."

All the kids yelled out at once with only some of them not in perfect unison, "Hello, Eira!"

"Hello, everyone." She waved, blushing at all the attention from the little wide eyes.

She looked at each one. They all seemed to be cuter than the next in their white robes that none seemed to fit, as they swallowed them whole.

"I expect you all to make me look really good in front of her, okay?"

"Yes, Sensei Ryu!" they all screamed out.

Usually, Eira disliked being around children, as they couldn't really control their instinct to look at her burns, but all these children were too excited to learn from Ryu to pay much attention to her. Thankfully, it stayed like that through the whole class, and it took Eira some effort not to laugh too much through the session when a child did something funny or adorable, like the one who took a tumble, falling to the ground when they tried to kick Ryu's hand as he held it out for a target. Each child had a different personality, and they all were beyond entertaining for the hour the session went on.

Both her and Ryu shared glances and small smiles throughout, and Eira couldn't have had a better time. She knew Ryu had been trying his best to convince her to stay on Kasumi Island ... and she had to admit it was kind of working.

At the end of their training, each child bowed to their sensei. Some kids left expeditiously, ready for their next activity, while some stayed to talk to Ryu. But there was one a beautiful little girl who went up to Eira, affectionately plopping right into her lap. Choppy, blunt bangs sat in the girl's eyes so much so that Eira had actually noticed her constantly trying her best to push them back during class.

"I'm Jun!" the girl exclaimed, unable to help herself from taking a piece of Eira's fiery-red hair and twirling it in her little chubby fingers.

Kids never seemed to care about personal space or the fact that Eira didn't like to be touched, but Eira didn't seem to mind at all. "Hi, Ju—"

"I love your hair." She couldn't even finish properly saying hi to the small child when the girl carried on talking.

Eira laughed. "Aw, thank you."

Jun kept twirling the strand, simply fascinated. "I've never seen red hair before."

"My mother, who used to live very far from here, is the one who passed it down to me."

"I bet your mommy is pretty like you."

"That's very sweet, Jun, thank you." Her heart warmed. Pulling the little girl closer into her, she touched the tip of her cute tiny nose. "You're very pretty, too."

Jun smiled widely that a girl as pretty as Eira would say that about her, but like all kids, she easily got distracted. When she noticed the flower in her hair, the envy in her eyes was obvious. "I love your flower."

"You do?" She asked, smiling, having forgotten about it and the fact her hair had been pulled back this whole time, revealing all her scars.

She hadn't even noticed Ryu had been watching her.

The girl bounced her head in a nod with her bangs bopping on her forehead.

Eira did what Ryu had earlier, pushing back Jun's hair and taking the flower from own her hair to place it above the little girl's ear. "It looks much better on you."

"Wow!" The girl's face lit up. "Thank you!"

"Come on, Jun," a woman who looked like an older Jun politely interrupted.

"Mom! Bye, Eira!"

With the girl flying off her lap in excitement, all Eira could do was yell back to her, "Bye, Jun!"

"Look at my pretty flower ..."

Eira chuckled at hearing Jun happily tell her mom about her day as they disappeared out the building.

She was alone now with Ryu, and the smirk on his face couldn't be missed.

"Told you," he gloated, grabbing his chest and pretending to be heartbroken. "And I'm appalled you didn't believe me."

Getting up from her spot, she walked over to him, playing into his dramatics with her own performance. "I'm big enough to admit I was wrong, and I apologize. Hopefully, this makes it all better." Leaning up on her tippytoes, she tenderly brushed her lips against his.

Appreciating her deep and fully meant sorrow for misjudging him, Ryu deepened the action by lifting her chin higher to let his tongue sweep hers up passionately.

In a fervent haze, she thought she could get used to days like this with Ryu when their kiss came to a sudden halt as they heard ...

The screams that only a mother could make in sheer terror.

24

DID I KILL JUN?

"What happened?" Ryu asked the screaming mother holding Jun. The beautiful, sweet girl lay limp in her arms, as if she had turned into a ragdoll.

"I-I don't know!" she cried out, trying to think under duress. "She was showing me her flower, and then ... and then ... she just dropped!"

Eira's heart sank at her words then fell to the pits of hell when her eyes caught the fallen bloodred flower she had given her. *What does she mean?! Did I kill Jun?*

But the old man, Ryu, and herself had all touched the flower, and they were fine.

When she went to pick it up to prove that couldn't possibly be it, Ryu stopped her.

"No! Don't touch it," he commanded as he quickly ripped a piece of cloth from his training robe.

"But it's just a flowe—"

"Could be, but I don't want to take any chances." He carefully used the cloth to grab it, then placed it in his pocket before taking Jun from her mother.

"Please help her!" the mother cried, knowing the king's son and her future king was her best hope.

"I will," he solemnly promised with a nod.

"She needs a doctor," Eira announced the obvious, and then was shocked when Ryu shook his head.

"No, she needs Itako," was all she heard as he took off running at a sprint.

Both Eira and the mother tried their bests to keep up with Ryu but lost him early on, as they heavily panted, out of breath. That was when Eira asked, confused, "Do you know who Itako is?"

The sobbing mother managed to speak. "She is a seeress."

She remembered the name now; it finally clicked in Eira's head that was who Ryu had sought to keep her from having nightmares. The vial he gave her to keep her asleep and dreamless had come from Itako.

But why would Ryu go to her? Eira knew better than to dare to voice her frustrations and doubt out loud to the mother, but she couldn't help her thoughts. *And that's going to save Jun how?*

As she followed the mother to the small house, she didn't know why, but she took the mother's hand in hers. "Maybe it's best if we wait out here." Inside couldn't be big enough for all of them, and it would be hard for Itako to think clearly with the child's mother crying and staring over their shoulder. "I know Ryu will do anything he can to save her."

Finally, the mother agreed with a whimpered sob.

Ryu entered the tiny home with a battle-ready Itako.

"Lay the child here."

Doing as ordered, he lay the small limp body down on the table in a rush, screaming, "How did you know? You could have fucking stopped thi—"

"I can only see what I am allowed to see, Ryu. I knew a child would be hurt, but I didn't know who or what did it," she said steadfast, trying to calm him and get to business while not the least bit offended. "Now, quickly, tell me what you know."

Instantly, Ryu calmed, knowing not only had he come to the right place, but that Itako hadn't just done nothing to intervene and save Jun's life. There was a healer on the island, a great one, but Ryu's gut had been telling him to see Itako, letting him know he needed to seek a different kind of help.

Carefully pulling out the thing in his pocket, he delicately unwrapped it for Itako, revealing the flower, only to see it was changing. "That's strange."

"What?" she asked.

"It was bloodred before, and full of life," Ryu explained the difference as best as he could. "Now, it's black and quickly dying."

Carefully, Itako took it in her hands and examined it. She began mumbling to herself, which seemed to be a fully one-sided conversation, as there was no one else there ...

Right? he thought, looking around.

Leaving Itako to whatever the hell she was doing, Ryu went up to the little girl and picked up her tiny hand that was turning cold.

Did I make the right decision? he questioned himself for what seemed like over a million times in a single second.

"Itako, she's dying," he warned gravely with tears

beginning to brim his eyes, trying to get her to hurry. Still, the old bat continued talking to herself.

Letting his head fall down over Jun's body, he did the only thing he thought was left and began to pray, to anyone or anything that would listen. He hoped some of his ancestral magic in him could help though he knew full well that wasn't how it worked, or his mother would still be alive. Nevertheless, he tried as he prayed over the girl's body.

When he felt Itako's presence move closer, he raised his head to shout at her but halted when he watched her pour a liquid into the lifeless mouth.

"What's that?" he asked through harsh tears, but it only took a few moments for him to get his answer when Jun started to warm in his hands as she was brought back to life.

The girl was weak at first and could only be heard saying, "Mommy ..."

Eira's heart sang when she saw a relieved Ryu waving them inside. The mother, who was now joined by Jun's father, ran inside, but Eira felt a bit nervous once she entered. Deciding to hold back, she stayed in the corner to watch.

She was grateful to see the sweet girl awake, and relief flooded her to her core. When she saw a teary-eyed Ryu, she felt for him. She only knew Jun for a few brief moments, but the child had entered Eira's own heart. She couldn't imagine how poor Jun's mother felt.

"She will be fine," Itako assured the weeping mother. "You may take her home to rest more comfortably."

"Thank you." Both parents cried, taking care in thanking both the seeress and Ryu.

"You have my life. If there's anything you ever need, let me know," the father said to them both.

Ryu bowed at him as he took his daughter in his arms before the happily crying family left.

With them gone, Itako wasted no time waving for her to come closer. "Come here, child."

Eira swallowed hard and somehow managed to slowly move forward. The old, frail woman was clearly blind, but when the withered hand reached out to touch the markings on her face, she didn't know how true that was.

Itako not only knew she was scarred, but she also hadn't stumbled trying to find which side of her face was marked, nor her burned hand that she now grabbed.

It was clear she was delighted to finally meet her. "Pretty."

Eira beamed with relief. "Thank you."

"That's it, child," Itako commented on her smile, confirming she was not as blind as she appeared. "For you no longer need to hide on this island. I see that Ryu has not told you about us ..."

Glancing over at Ryu, she wondered what in the world he had forgotten to mention to her this time.

"On this island, we do not see scars as weakness. We see them as proud badges of honor that many men and women here will be envious of." Itako firmly gripped her hands in hers tighter. "When things break, we do not throw them away. We put them back together and make them"— she now took Ryu's hand and placed it on top of Eira's— "stronger."

A grinning Ryu made Eira certain she had missed something, possibly an inside tale that only the two knew. However, Itako continued.

"Leaving this island would be a mistake, child, for you have yet to finish your metamorphosis. Give it just one more day"—she lifted a frail finger—"for you might be surprised what can change in just another sunrise."

Even though Eira had no plans of staying after this ordeal, she could agree to just one more night. "All right."

"Good." Satisfied she would stay, Itako shooed them away. "Now go. It is naptime."

They turned to leave the tiny house, but the seeress quickly remembered something.

"Oh, and Ryu ... I'll be seeing you later."

When they finally left, Eira couldn't help but ask, "What does Itako mean?"

But he was clearly just as confused as Eira. "Something tells me I'll find out later."

25

WAKE THE DEAD

Ryu had taken Eira straight to the palace. There was a tingling of uneasiness that pricked at his mind ... That flower had been meant for her, not Jun.

Kasumi Island and his people were peaceful. It was an unmarred place of violence, and it was why they had kept the island secret for an eternity. Rarely, its people left, and even rarer were they banished, like Kenshi had been. Yet Eira had barely escaped death today.

With her now safe, Ryu wasted no time slipping back out to where the old man had given her the flower earlier. The house that was closest to the spot, he was certain belonged to the man, so he didn't bother to knock. It had been strange to know exactly what he would find before he even opened the door.

With the old man lying cold on the floor with a dried-up flower in his hand, Ryu only had one thought in his mind.

Good riddance.

Ryu found himself at Itako's later in the night, just like she had said. Of course, he hadn't known earlier why he would be here, and it wasn't until Eira had fallen asleep, crying over how their day had gone, that he'd realized what must be done.

Eira felt all alone on a foreign land, but it wasn't her home that she missed, as it had done nothing but betray her ... it was her grandparents.

And as much as Ryu didn't *particularly* want them to come over, he knew it needed to be done if Kasumi Island was going to begin to feel like home for her.

Itako sat in her rocking chair next to her empty fireplace, smoking her pipe. She didn't even bother to wait to hear his voice, knowing exactly who had entered.

"Is he dead?"

"He is," he confirmed. "But shouldn't you know?" She was a seeress, after all.

She didn't miss a beat, having no love lost at the islander's death. "I speak to the dead, but I cannot speak to the ones where he went."

Ryu's skin turned icy at her words.

"Ask your question ..." She could sense there was something on his mind, and it was true. He had been wondering something all day.

"How come nothing happened to me and Eira? We both touched the flower."

"The flower isn't deadly by touch but *by smell*," she answered all knowingly.

"So, Jun smelled the flower when she left," he mumbled

the obvious under his breath. Now it all made sense, and why he had found the man dead by the second flower. "But why would he want to kill Eira?"

"People only harm for two reasons"—her grave voice echoed her wisdom—"either to attain power or to feel powerful."

Ryu knew she was right. He highly doubted the old man could possibly think he could attain power. Therefore, he must've wanted to feel powerful, like Kenshi, and so he hoped his problem was already solved.

"Now"—the old witch got to the point of why he had really come, using the sucking end of her pipe to point to the table where the little girl had lain on earlier—"what you seek is over there."

Ryu went over to find two little bottles full of shiny, golden elixir. "Why didn't you give these to me earlier?"

"Who's to say you would have come to the same conclusion if I gave them to you earlier?"

All this made his brain hurt, so he decided to leave it. He'd never understand why Itako did the things she did in the order she did them.

"Will this work?"

She simply shrugged. "I suppose you're going to find out."

"So, you don't know if it will?" The frustration over her riddles was evident in his voice.

"My ancestors have told me they have tried to bring lovers over before, but nothing worked." It happened from time to time; an islander would leave to see the outside world only for them to fall in love. It always ended cruelly, as they could never bring their lover over to their homeland and were then forced to choose between the love of their life or love of their home.

Ryu lost a bit more of his composure. "And exactly why do you think it will now?"

"They were not me," she sneered with pride.

Placing them in his pocket, he supposed that bit was true. If there was one thing he didn't doubt with Itako, it was her knowledge and power.

"Also, they share blood with Eira, whereas others did not share it with anyone here. I'm hopeful *that* will be the difference."

Now Ryu fully understood, and it was enough for him to turn to leave, knowing it might work.

"If I don't see you anytime soon," she drawled before he could disappear, "I know it worked."

Stopping in his tracks, he smiled. "But you always know if I will see you again."

"I do," Itako confirmed.

"And do you see me returning?" he asked.

Putting the pipe to her lips with a smile, she didn't utter a word.

Ryu had expected to feel happiness at her smile, but it made him oddly sad to think he wouldn't be seeing the bitch anytime soon. And while his heart grew a bit fond of her, he was sure he'd regret his next words.

"Would you like me to start a fire?"

Itako blew out a puff of smoke. "I thought you'd never ask."

It took him only a moment to figure out he had been had. "That's why you didn't give me the bottles earlier, isn't it?"

The blind lady no longer left any pretenses. "Yep."

"Get in the boat!" Ryu found himself screaming at the second old lady he'd encountered tonight.

"It's too small for all three of us," the old lady spat back, sticking her heels into the rocky terrain.

It was the boat he had taken before Eira had known he was a dragon, when he had left and come back from his island to help with Eira's nightmares. He wasn't quite sure, but he was a little sure everything on his island held a little magic, so it shouldn't sink. Or so he hoped.

He regretted this mission and was thinking about turning into his dragon form and disappearing right this second, but it was too late when the supposed arthritis-eaten fisherman got in the boat with ease, as if he was back in his golden days. If he shifted now, he'd kill him. And while it felt like that wouldn't be such a bad thought in this moment, his conscience won out.

Taking the white box from Eira's grandmother's hands that he knew the contents of all too well, he put it in the grandfather's lap before he faced the stubborn grandmother.

Knowing he was left with one, and only one, option, he leaned down and swung her over his shoulder before placing her in the middle of the tiny boat.

"Shut up!" the grandfather shouted. "If I can hear you that loud, you're going to wake the whole town up!"

She paused her shrilling at the drop of a hat to turn around and hit her husband. "Oh, please! I'm not that loud!"

"Could have fooled me, woman," he ground out back at his wife. "You could wake the dead!"

Ryu wasted no time using their argument as his distraction to get the boat in the water, pushing them out as deep as he could before he climbed into the boat and started rowing.

It only took the grandmother a few moments to notice she was now stuck. "You know, if I had known you'd be taking my granddaughter across the ocean in some shitty boat, I wouldn't have let her go."

"Don't worry," Ryu assured her with a sly smile, "we didn't go by boat."

Even more concern grew on her wise face. "Then how did you ...? Is Eira all right?"

He decided to take a page from Itako's book. "You'll find out soon enough and can ask her all your questions then."

Ryu hoped that would be enough to suffice for a quiet boat ride and was worried it wouldn't, until all concern left the grandmother's face. It seemed she knew something when she grabbed the box from her husband's lap.

"Did you know the prison system sends a letter to the victims when their attacker dies?"

Ryu sat silent, quietly rowing.

"I only brought this box so no one else could find it, since you said we couldn't return. But ..." Seeing they were far from the shore, she reached inside to take out the framed picture of her lost son, daughter-in-law, and young Eira before the grandmother tossed the box into the ocean while she watched all its horrid contents sink to its depths. "It's time we *all* move on."

Proudly, Ryu nodded his head, now knowing why that worry had left her face, as it was clear to her that Ryu wouldn't do anything to ever hurt Eira.

Suddenly, there was a silent, blissful understanding between the two. However, it lasted only a moment ...

"So, how did you and Eira get across?" she quipped.

Rowing faster, he spoke with clenched teeth, "Just hope this boat is big enough that you don't have to find out."

With that, the couple stayed silently, praying the rest of the way.

26
A WHAT?

"Where'd you go?" she asked with swollen eyes. It had been the second time Ryu had slipped away from her last night, and she hadn't gotten much sleep because she'd sat up, worried about where he had gone in the middle of the night.

"I have something to show you."

Eira was shocked by his excitement. "What?"

"It's a surprise."

After what happened yesterday and him being out all through the night, she wasn't sure where this could go, so she decided to remind him about the last surprise that had ended with her being flown over the ocean. "I didn't like the first one."

"This one, I think you'll like," he assured her with a certain smirk.

"Ryu ..."

"Yes," he answered, grumbling, knowing something bothered her.

"Did you ...? Did you ...?" She couldn't even bear to say it.

"No," Ryu answered honestly, seeming to read her mind.

She let relief flood her for only a moment before he continued.

"But it wasn't from lack of trying. He was already dead when I got there." Leaving no pretenses that he would have done it, his savage voice held no hint of remorse. "I would have made him the third death for you."

Eira swallowed with her eyes practically bulging out of her head. "*Third?*"

"Sorry—" Ryu quickly spoke to correct himself. "I meant second."

"Oh." Eira didn't know if he was telling the truth or not, but he had to have been because no one besides Kenji had turned up dead.

Yet ...

Getting a headache from her ruthless dragon and her traitorous thoughts, she supposed a speech about not killing was in order. But it was Ryu, which meant there was a one percent chance of him *actually* listening.

Sadness at the thought of the old man who had given her that flower filled her. She couldn't believe he had tried to hurt her, but something gnawed at her. "Do you think he knew it was harmful?"

It was obvious by Ryu's expression that he found the question odd. "The way I found him dead tells me he did."

"Oh," she whispered in defeat, understanding how he had perished. "You don't think someone *else* might try something, too?"

"No, I don't think so." He thoughtfully shook his head. "Our people are peaceful. I know, with Kenshi and the old man, it might not seem like it, but we are."

Only because Ryu was so certain did Eira relax.

Everyone was much nicer here on Kasumi Island, that much was true.

Instead of pressing further, she wanted to move on from the depressing topic. "So, what's the surpri—" The sound of yelling coming through the door made her pause.

"Fuck," he exasperated before running off.

What the—

She ran after him, as it seemed his surprise was downstairs and, in fact, backfiring. The screaming got louder with each step she took down the giant staircase and toward the foyer, and she thought she recognized the voice for a moment.

Is that ...?

No, it couldn't be.

Could it?

"Who the hell are you?" Tatsu was heard screaming.

The old man spat back right at his face, "Well, who the hell are you?"

"Yeah, we know who *we are*, but who are you?" the old lady backed her husband.

"*This is my house!*" Tatsu roared at the loons. "Now, for the last time, who the hell are yo—"

Oh my God—

"Grandmother!" Eira somehow got past Ryu and jumped into her grandmother's arms to make sure it wasn't an illusion.

"Hey, honey, nice to see you, but I'm kinda in the middle of something." She patted her before squaring up with Tatsu again.

Ryu coughed, getting all their attention, while the regret on his face was visible. "These are Eira's grandparents, and this is my father, Tatsu."

"You have a lovely home, Tatsu." Grandmother beamed,

doing a full one-eighty now with the introductions that clearly sent Ryu's father over the edge.

Grandfather didn't help his attitude by picking up an expensive chachki.

Tatsu's mouth dropped open at the audacity, then it thinned into a firm line before he snatched the item out of the grubby hands and set the precious item carefully back in its place. He then focused his frustrations on the source of his new problem. His son.

"How in the hell did you get them over here? It's impossibl—" It was obvious the moment he said it, he figured out how. With anger and disgust, he cursed the name, "Itako."

They all watched him storm off toward the front door.

"Where are you going?" Ryu dared to ask the obvious.

"She's going to undo what she has done," Tatsu promised.

His son scratched his head. "I don't think it works like that."

"Watch me," his father said, slamming the door shut with finality.

Grandmother wasted no time once he was gone. "What's up his butt?"

Ryu simply pinched the bridge of his nose, clearly debating his life choices.

Seeing his patience was wearing thin, Eira decided to change the subject. "How did you get here?" She was still so in shock at seeing them that it felt almost like a dream. The way Ryu had explained it, it was impossible, just like Tatsu had said.

"We got here by boat. A very small one, I might add," Grandmother noted, displeased. "But how in the world did you get here?"

Eira looked over at Ryu, stunned by the question. "*You*

haven't told them yet?" she whispered to him, but obviously, not so well.

"Told us what?" they asked in not so deaf unison. Even Grandfather, who had picked up the chachki again with Tatsu gone, had gotten closer, clearly wanting to know the secret. It was funny how he could choose what he wanted to hear and what he didn't.

"Grandmother, Grandfather …" she choked out before finally croaking out Ryu's secret with his nodded approval. "Ryu's a dragon."

The precious item in Grandfather's hand went crashing to the floor. "*A what?*"

27

GROW OLD WITH ME

Entering her bedroom after she finally got her grandparents settled in for the night, she was happy to find Ryu already in bed. "I can't believe you did that for me," she said breathlessly and with a smile. "That was very kind of you."

"Of course." He lifted his lips in his own smile. "Anything to make you happy, darling."

She knew he, in fact, meant it, considering who her grandparents were, but ugh, she had to admit whenever he used that term of endearment, her stomach did somersaults.

Quickly, she got ready for bed. After spending the whole day with her grandparents, she had missed Ryu, and now the fire inside burned with a passion to get close to him. She was worried he had fallen asleep until she crawled into bed and his lashes lifted.

She snuggled close to him under the covers, but her body cried out for her to somehow get even closer.

"You know, she told me everything you had to do to get her here, but I have one question ..."

"What's that?" he asked, dragging her into his arms tighter. It was obvious he felt much the same way as she did at the moment.

"How did you get her in the boat?"

Ryu belly-laughed so hard it shook her. "It wasn't easy."

"I imagine so." She chuckled with him, seeing the mental image in her mind. It was a wonder everyone had gotten to the island alive.

With their laughter dying, Eira wanted to properly thank him. "Thank you, Ryu. I can't tell you what it means that you did that for me." Bringing her face closer to his in the lamp's light glow, she gave him a slow-burning kiss in return for his kindness.

Still clearly mesmerized, he asked. "That's all? It was a *very* small boat, you know."

Smiling, Eira repeated her kiss, giving him more this time. Her own body wanted to deepen it as well, so she slipped her tongue into his warm mouth, and it was as if she ignited an inferno.

Ryu felt the ignite, too, letting himself explore her mouth hotly. He then left her lips to trail a kiss to her ear then her neck. As he traveled down a little bit lower, Eira didn't dare it to end; she went for the buttons of her top, hoping Ryu wouldn't stop her this time.

He didn't.

Letting her drift her top away, he captured one of her pretty nipples before his tongue swirled over his new precious artifact. After taking his time caring for one, he then showed the same interest to the other.

Eira was certain if she could combust, this was it, that she would implode at any moment. Yet it was only the beginning. She felt as if her next breath could be her last, so how were they supposed to even complete their mating?

If she had ignited the fire, Ryu did everything in the power of his mouth to make it go ablaze. So, when his mouth left her skin, she thought she would burst into tears.

"What are you doing?" she whimpered when he buttoned her blouse back up.

"You need rest," was all the excuse he gave before placing a kiss on her cheek. "Sleep."

What? Did he not feel that? How in the world was she supposed to sleep after *that*?

Her exasperation only grew, yet Ryu turned over and went right to sleep like what they had just shared was nothing. *How can he sleep after that?*

It was only when she tossed and turned for almost half an hour, that she heard him say, "Are you okay?"

"Do you not feel"—she waved her hand between them, not able to find the words at a moment when her blood boiled like lava under her skin, even though, on the outside, she looked completely normal—"t*his*?"

Was she crazy? He shouldn't've even let himself have a taste of her ...

Yet he couldn't help himself. *Could I?*

"Of course I feel it." Ryu's hoarse voice almost cracked, and when he could tell she didn't believe his words, he pulled her closer to him so she could feel for herself.

Lying in his arms, she could feel the heat that seared

under his skin, like hers, but there was something else entirely as she could practically feel the vibrations coming off him.

"Oh." His father had been right. It was obvious the dragon felt way more of their bond than she did. "But why did you stop?" she breathed, unbelieving he would keep himself in this pain.

Finally, he told her the selfless truth, "Your body and our mating are only telling you that you are ready, and in this life, I don't want you to ever doubt why you are with me, fated mate or not."

After his profound words sent her heart into a frenzy, she intently listened to the strong, constant thumping of his heart as she rested her head on his chest until her heart began to beat with his. The beautiful melody as they beat together in harmony practically put her into a contended sleep.

It had been a long time since Eira had felt safe and protected, but she had never felt sheer love and adoration like this from someone who wasn't family.

And it was completely reciprocated.

With a yawn, she gave in to sleep only a moment after she voiced her revelation. "I love you, Ryu."

Even though he knew she was fast asleep, he would tell her in her dreamless dream what he had known from the moment he had met her. "And I love you, darling."

The next day, Ryu had taken the opportunity, when her grandparents were busy settling in, to take Eira for a walk.

They walked hand in hand, yet she had no idea where they were going. *Again.*

As they took their journey, Eira had to admit the island was officially growing on her. There was nothing left for her anywhere else, and all the important people in her life were here, as well as some new ones. She felt a serene peace for once. Like the weight of her scars had finally been lifted.

"Are we close?" she asked when they were no longer passing homes but fields. Was the island bigger than it appeared from her cliff?

"Just a bit further."

She was certain the island was when they went further out in the fields that were sprouting.

"You see, we are known for growing this on the island," Ryu began, bending down to dig up a sprouted plant and handing it to her.

Eira recognized it immediately as the root she would get from Kenji at his cart.

"It's customary, when someone finds a person they want to spend the rest of their life with, to come here and pick a root to take it back and give to their lover as a gift and a promise of what they hope to build together in the future."

Her heart pounded, understanding two things all over-whelmingly at once.

That this root did mean something secretly to Kenji, like Ryu had said.

And secondly, what it meant for him to bring her here and tell her this.

When she continued staring down at the root in disbelief, Ryu lifted her chin with a strong finger to force her gaze to his. "Eira ..."

She bit her lip in anticipation.

"Do you want to grow old with me," Ryu finally asked with a charming smile, "slowly?"

28

YOU KNOW HOW MEN ARE

They all sat around the dinner table, raising their glasses to the happy couple. It had only been a few days since Ryu had asked her to marry him, and everything was happening so fast that it was starting to give Eira butterflies and whiplash all at once.

After the toast, Ryu's father stood proudly. "Eira, there is something I'd like to give you, as it is customary here for the families to exchange gifts."

"Oh, sorry," Grandmother blurted out rather unregretfully. "We don't have a gift."

Tatsu paused only for a moment to roll his eyes, not the least bit surprised by the outburst. Then, the moment after he snapped his fingers, someone entered with a huge box and set it in front of Eira.

As she slowly opened it and peeled back the paper, she noticed a bright white garment beautifully preserved.

"It's what my Kana wore on our wedding day many moons ago. She wanted to be sure to save everything for our son's future wife, so even the jewelry she wore is in there."

"Wow," Eira breathed. The dress was breathtaking. She could see the love and just how much it had been cherished with the care it had been packed with. "Thank you." She beamed with a glistening in her eyes that matched Tatsu's. If there was one thing for certain about Ryu's father, it was how obviously he loved his late wife.

"I have something for you, too," Yuri announced with a warm smile, handing Eira her own beautifully wrapped, small package.

Both she and her father, Kage, had grown close to Ryu, as Kage was his sensei. The many years of training he'd spent with him had naturally bound the two in friendship, and Kage appeared to be his one and only true friend on the island.

And now it was Eira who considered Yuri to be her one and only true friend here. Well, for someone who wasn't her grandparents or Ryu. The girls had grown close quickly in a short amount of time, and Yuri had become one of the people Eira didn't want to live without.

"Aw, Yuri. You didn't have to," she said, unwrapping the gift to reveal a small and delicate perfume bottle. "Thank you, that's very kind of you."

"Very kind," Tatsu agreed with a nod.

Unable to wait to smell it, she went to open the bottle, hoping she was going to be able to smell even half as amazing as Yuri did all the time. It was a kind and thoughtful gift that Eira never thought to get for herself, so she would cherish it forever.

"Let it be a surprise on your big day. It's good luck to wear a new perfume in the beginning of your new life," Yuri said, placing her hand over Eira's before she could open it. "Here, let me take your gifts up to your room for you."

Smiling, Eira agreed it would be better to wait. "Thank you, Yuri. I know I'll love it."

"Okay, now, where were we?" Tatsu said now that the gifts had been exchanged.

"Hopefully, at the part where we can finally eat." Her grandfather's frustrated grumble under his breath wasn't missed.

Ignoring his unfavorable guests, Ryu's father continued, "It's also tradition for the bride's second dress for the dinner to match the color of her mate's dragon. Since my dragon was red, Kana's dress simply won't due. You'll need a gold one."

Grandmother's brow lifted. "Gold, you say?"

Hearing soft sobs come from her closet, Eira lightly pushed the door open to find a missing Yuri crying on her large closet floor.

"Yuri ... what's wrong?"

"I'm so sorry, Eira. Please don't hate me."

"Oh, Yuri!" Worry encased Eira from witnessing her friend's distress. She hurried over to where Yuri sat on the ground and thankfully didn't notice her hurt or anything alarming, besides the fear on Yuri's face that told her something was amiss. "I could never hate you. What happened?"

"I was just stowing away your gifts, and when I went to put away the necklace Tatsu gave you, it ... it broke," she muttered before finally revealing the broken necklace between her hands.

A sigh of relief escaped her, having feared much worse.

"That's not your fault, Yuri. I'm sure it's very old. Ryu and Tatsu will understan—"

When Yuri broke into uncontrollable cries, Eira could barely make out her words.

"Tatsu will fire me for breaking something of his late wife's."

"I'm sure there's time to get it fix—"

Her cries only grew louder. "Not for something this precious. It will take time. Your wedding is only days away!"

Eira bit her lip, trying to think through Yuri's tears. Why did they have to get married so fast? But then she quickly remembered Ryu's pain and her own needs growing immensely each day, telling her exactly why.

Pushing those thoughts away at a time like this, she got back to focusing on the matter at hand. "I bet they won't even notice. He gave me so many things to wear." She shrugged like it was nothing before trying her best to make light of the situation to cheer the poor girl up. "You know how men are."

Yuri sniffled. "And if they do?"

Her silence was deafening, as Eira came up empty for what they could do.

"I'll be gone!" Yuri's waterworks began again. "I might as well pack my bags now."

Eira didn't think so at all, as it seemed Tatsu much preferred Yuri over her, which was understandable since he barely knew her. Then again, it was a belonging of his late wife's, and if Yuri believed him to do something that cruel, then she didn't want to risk it. Losing her only girlfriend on this island would hurt Eira too much.

"I—" Eira struggled for her brave words to announce themselves. "I will tell them I broke it."

Her friend looked at her in disbelief. "You ... would do that for me?"

"Of course, I would," Eira confirmed with finality. "And I will."

All the tears on Yuri's face suddenly dried up as she grabbed her friend to hold her dearly. "Oh, Eira, thank you!"

"No problem. It's not like they'd kick me out ..." she said, patting her back, gulping nervously. It seemed her bravery wavered to her nerve. "Right?"

29

BOUND

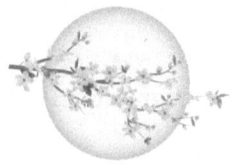

Tensely waiting for the marriage ceremony to begin, Eira twisted her hands together to prevent herself from smoothing them over the front of her solid white kimono. Not wanting handprints to mar the beauty of the garment she had been gifted only made it more difficult to resist.

"Why are you so nervous?" Her grandmother took her hands, stopping the twisting movements. "If you don't want to marry Ryu, I will have your grandfather steal a boat, and we will return home."

Eira thought her grandmother looked excited—more excited about her possibly running away from the marriage than her going through with the ceremony. But she had to burst her bubble that she would have to see Tatsu again and try her best to get along. *Hopefully.*

"I want to marry Ryu, Grandmother."

Shoulders slumped in disappointment, Grandmother said, "Perhaps it will be better if your grandfather and I leave after the ceremo—"

"No." Eira stopped those blasphemous thoughts. She

was about to have everything the girl before her accident, and the girl she had become after, ever wanted, and she wasn't about to lose it. "I want you and Grandfather to stay … Ryu and Tatsu will grow on you." Again, *hopefully.*

"Ryu, sure. Tatsu, not so much." Her grandmother sniffed, as if holding back tears. "I believe in the old ways as well, but he is prehistoric."

Eira didn't think she was necessarily wrong, but she needed to keep the peace and could only hope she sounded surer than she felt.

"We will all learn to live harmoniously together."

Taking a deep breath, trying to believe her own words, she couldn't help but wonder if Tatsu was trying to convince Ryu not to marry her like her grandmother was her. Did their marriage stand a chance with so many against their match?

From where they were waiting, she was able to look out at the sacred Sakura tree. Nearly a thousand beautiful streamers of gold, red, and pink adorned the tree, making it look simply magical as they filled the tree to make it full once more. The ones hung on lower branches spiraled down to the ground with only a small opening for them to wed under. Everything was ready, except Tatsu and Ryu had yet to make their appearance so the ceremony could begin.

Releasing her hands, her grandmother removed something from her kimono to place into her hands. "This was my mother's."

Eira stared down at the delicately intricate fan. Flipping it open, she had to blink back tears. It was the same heirloom she had seen her mother holding in a picture of her parents' wedding. "I can't believe—"

"It is to bring happiness to your marriage, and you're

going to need all the luck you can get." Her grandmother, as always, brushed off the sentimental moment.

Eira would have been hurt if she had not seen the suspicious glimmer of tears in the wise eyes.

"Thank you."

With the reminder of luck, she remembered Yuri's perfume that she had forgotten to wear. "Give me a few minutes. I forgot someth—"

All of a sudden, her grandmother huffed out a sigh of relief, stopping her. "You don't have time."

Eira looked to where she was staring, to see Tatsu had taken his place under the tree, as he would be the one to perform the ceremony, making her completely forget about the gift all over again.

"I guess Tatsu couldn't talk him out of marrying you," Grandmother noted as Ryu finally took his place as well.

"I suppose not," she said with her own relieved smile that she hid behind her fan.

Taking the cue, her grandmother went to the curtained-off wall. "Ready?"

Keeping her fan up to cover the lower half of her face, Eira took one last deep breath before she nodded and hoped she sounded as brave as she felt when she said, "Ready."

With slumped shoulders, withered hands pulled the curtain open to hear gasps from the small amount of seated guests.

Frightened, Eira took her first few steps alone as she clung to her fan for dear life, grateful that it could conceal her nerves. Once she reached the curtained entrance, her grandmother joined her in taking the final steps of ending her old life and starting anew.

She kept her head lowered, too nervous to meet Ryu's gaze once she reached the end of the aisle and took her place. She slowly lifted her eyes over her fan as she told herself if she didn't see love for her in Ryu's eyes, she wouldn't complete the wedding ceremony.

When his gaze met hers unflinchingly, her doubts of Ryu not wanting to marry her fled under his loving gaze. So, she stayed put as the beautiful ceremony began and they bound themselves to each other before all their loved ones.

It was a short, sweet, and warm ceremony, and before she knew it, Ryu was reminding her to lower her fan.

Once she put it away, Eira was unable to keep her heart from doing a happy dance at the way Ryu took her into his arms to seal their marriage with a kiss.

Their kiss, much like their ceremony, left her pleased and content. Joy erupted from their few guests, and even Eira could see the pure happiness on Ryu's father's face as he introduced the new couple. It heartened her to know that Tatsu clearly hadn't been trying to persuade his son against the marriage and, in fact, wholeheartedly meant it when he had blessed them.

When she was finally able to see their guests' faces, she met the same joy, until her eyes skimmed over Kage's.

Struck at the hatred, which was gone just as soon as it had appeared, she wondered if she had imagined it as they walked away together.

"Come, Eira. You need to get changed for the reception," her grandmother said, reminding her that they were on a strict schedule.

Ryu gave his bride a quick kiss on the cheek, clearly thinking it was still wedding nerves. "See you soon, darling."

Pulling herself out of Ryu's arms, she avoided his gaze, still stunned at the hatred she had witnessed on Kage's face.

Eira followed her grandmother to the room she had just left and changed into the more elaborate gold kimono that had belonged to her grandmother. Ryu had flown back over to retrieve it from the back of her grandmother's dusty closet. Tiny flowers and cranes had been embroidered with gold threads. As she stared in the mirror, she was almost afraid to wear the priceless garment.

"Turn around." Her grandmother mopped her cheeks with the sleeve of her kimono, staring at her proudly. "How I wish your mother and father could see you."

Swallowing her own tears at the reminder of her parents, she turned back to the mirror to take it all in. "Me, too."

"You look too pretty to cry." Her grandmother stopped her from ruining her looks by distracting her with something else. "Here, don't forget this."

Turning away from the mirror, she saw a silver dagger in her grandmother's hand and allowed her to hide it in special pocket, which had been sewn into her kimono. The dagger was a symbol of protection for her family.

She didn't feel comfortable having the dagger on her, but her grandmother was determined she carry out the old traditional customs that she herself had followed.

She couldn't help but laugh. "And you say Tatsu is prehistoric."

"Oh, hush," Grandmother shushed, refusing to admit she was anything like Ryu's father.

Stifling her laughter, Eira placed the fan in the belt of her kimono when Ryu knocked before entering to take her to the dinner portion of their wedding.

She blushed at the admiring way he looked at her once her grandmother had left them to have a moment alone. He was wearing the same gold kimono, which had a white lining. On the front, his family's crest of a dragon had been embroidered with the same gold thread. He looked so handsome that she had to flip her fan open to fan herself.

"My wife looks absolutely beautiful," Ryu breathed as he held out his arm so she could wind hers around him.

"You look good yourself, husband," she complimented back with a twinkle at using their new titles.

"Our guests are waiting," He had to tell not only her but himself so they could get to the dinner. "We can admire each other tonight."

Happy she could use the fan to cover her red cheeks, she held on to his arm tightly as he escorted her.

She felt as if her heart was as heavy as her kimono as they walked toward the reception room. On the tables were origami cranes, each folded differently and of various colors. Dozens of low tables with pillows surrounding them were placed around the room. Unlike for the ceremony, the whole island had been invited.

When she spotted Kage as they took their places for dinner, she found no hint of malice, making her wonder if the falling sun had played a trick of light on his face. *That must be it.*

As she let any worry about Ryu's friend and sensei leave her, guests already began approaching to congratulate the couple. One in particular brought a smile to each of their faces as they watched the old lady shuffle closer to them.

"I was honored to be one of the few to see you wed." Itako bowed. "But I have to tell you, Eira, that you looked absolutely regal. Kana would have been proud to see you wearing her dress."

"Thank you, Itako." Eira bowed, not knowing how the supposed blind seeress could see her wearing it, but nonetheless, she was glad for her to have witnessed it. The lady had come to mean a lot to Ryu's and her love story.

"Yes, we can't thank you enough for coming," Ryu agreed with his own respectful bow.

"Well, I couldn't miss not only a fated mate wedding but a soulmate one, nonetheless."

A stunned Eira was clearly so confused that even the blind seeress could pick it up.

"What?"

"I better take my seat." Itako smiled, sensing Ryu's frustration at her bomb-dropping words. "There are other guests waiting to give you their best wishes of health and happiness. You two have quite a *long* night ahead of you." And with a wink, she left.

"Ryu ..." Eira had missed the innuendo, still stuck on Itako's previous words. "What does she mean by soulmate?"

"Pay that old witch no mind." Ryu shrugged, clearly regretting her special invite. "She's crazy."

30

I CAN'T PROMISE NOT TO EAT YOU

The water fell from the ceiling like raindrops. Lifting her face toward it, she tried to forget Ryu was waiting for her. She had lead weight in her stomach, which she couldn't blame on the amount of food she had eaten at their wedding celebration. As she had sat next to Ryu, she had been aware of the low whispers from the tables.

She was not one of them.

She felt every islander's sights on her, each of their gazes flickering over her like a flame on her skin, burning away what confidence she had until each dish she tried tasted like ash in her mouth. She much preferred their ceremony over the dinner, and it wasn't until the end that she started to understand the importance of Ryu's people to be included.

The mother and father of Jun had stood up, not only to wish happiness to the newlyweds in their new lives together, but they thanked them for their actions in saving their daughter's life. Each islander had stood after their words and bowed lowly before them in not only respect but adoration.

That was when she finally relaxed enough to hear the whisperings were not about the scars that marred her but of how beautiful their future queen looked and how proud they were to welcome her to their island. And as the rest of the celebration continued, Eira's confidence grew more and more ...

Well, until they reached the confines of their bedroom, alone. Then all confidence shot out of her as she ran to the bathroom for a few moments of deep breathing that turned into a much-needed shower.

Toweling off, she pulled on a white silken nightgown that was so exquisite she was afraid to put it on. As she brushed her fiery hair, she listened to what Ryu was doing in the other room. Had she taken so many moments that he had gone to sleep?

After straightening the bathroom, she took another five minutes and was about to step out of the bathroom when she remembered the perfume.

There was an assortment of scents to choose from on the vanity that she had never thought to use before. She would never get used to having all her needs taken care of by Ryu and his staff. Each of the bottles looked so pretty that it was hard to decide which one to choose.

Her hand hovered over the see-through, red-colored bottle of perfume that Yuri had given her as a present. When Yuri had hugged her earlier, she had noticed the scent was missing, and when Eira had told her that she had forgotten it and wanted to go back to get it but couldn't as the ceremony was about to begin, Yuri had simply smiled at her friend before whispering, only to her ears, that it was actually better that she waited to use it on her wedding night, as it would increase Ryu's desire for her.

Yep, she was going to give that a hard pass.

Choosing a pale amber frosted perfume bottle, which had hummingbirds on the outside, she opened it to place a small amount on her neck. The subtle fragrance was exactly what she wanted—she didn't want Ryu roused from his sleep because of a strong scent.

Not able to come up with anything else to delay the inevitable, she finally stepped out of the room.

Ryu was sitting up in the bed, staring at the door with an expression that had her tummy doing flip flops, but it was simply too late to turn back now.

Maybe not? She wrung her hands and started to turn around.

"Eira." His deep voice stopped her in her tracks. "Where are you going?"

"I forgot something in the bathroom," she told him shakily.

"What did you forget?"

Grumbling her confession under her breath, she wished she had never left the safe confines. "To stay there."

Ryu softly patted the bed beside him. "Come here, darling."

Swallowing a gulp, which he might have heard, considering the frown that formed on his forehead, she slowly walked toward the bed.

"You know I would never hurt you, Eira."

She sat down on the edge of the bed, putting as much distance between them as possible.

"I'm just curious—" She started to ask but had to clear her throat when she heard the fear in her voice. "There isn't a chance you'll lose control and change into a dragon when we're ... you know ...?"

"Making love?" Ryu offered the words she couldn't seem to form.

"Yes." She had to clear her throat again. "Making love."

However, he was not appeased with her pretend bravery.

"It would be nice if you didn't sound as if you were about to walk to the guillotine."

Was Ryu aware that when he became frustrated, she could see the reflection of his dragon in his eyes?

Scooting a bit closer to him so he wouldn't think she was such a child, she confessed her worries, "I'm not worried about being beheaded. I'm afraid you'll flambé or eat me."

Ryu's expression gentled after hearing her legitimate concerns. He ran an even gentler finger just under the neckline of her gown. "I'm not going to be able to make any promises, as I expect there to be a lot of fire when we make love." His wicked smile had her insides suddenly quivering. "And I can't promise not to eat you."

She stared at him, too paralyzed to jump up from the bed when he kissed the throbbing pulse at the base of her throat. "You won't?" she asked huskily as she was reminded of the pull and need that had been overtaken by her nerves from knowing that tonight was the night and there was no longer a reason to delay their mating.

"Nope," he growled out in a sensual tone that curled her toes. "But you can bite me back, and I won't complain."

"You're playing with me, aren't you?" A small giggle escaped her, which had her hand covering the silly noise.

"No ..." Lowering one sleeve of her gown, Ryu kissed her

bare shoulder as he pulled her down onto the bed with him. "You look so beautiful."

Looking into his eyes, she could no longer see his dragon's reflection but her face. Humbly, she wondered if that was really the way he saw her. With him, she did feel beautiful, as if they were not only fated mates but soulmates, too, like Itako had said ... *were they?*

Any thoughts she had just obtained whispered away as Ryu rolled onto his side and leaned on his elbow to gaze upon her. When his hand lay upon her belly, he started bunching up the nightgown, and it not only tugged the nightgown downward at the neckline, but it also rose from her ankles.

"That's a slick move," she told him.

"I'm glad you approve."

Raising a brow, she gave him a disapproving look. "Depends on how you learned that trick."

"I must have learned it in another lifetime."

She wasn't taken in by his innocent front, nor had she picked up the hint of his words, too enthralled by his eyes that remained on her chest as the gown slowly lowered to expose her breasts until they were naked beneath his dragon-like raptor gaze.

She jumped when his tongue circled her nipple, but the hand at her waist kept her on the bed. His breath felt hot on her flesh. Instead of frightening her, the sensations fanned her own flame of desire.

Surprised at how quickly Ryu was raising her passion, the word *soulmates* entered her mind, making her wonder if they were not only fated mates in this life but perhaps soulmates in *every* life ...

Belief began to fill her as Ryu began making love to her for the first time, but the sensations were too familiar. This wasn't only the second time he had covered her nipple with his mouth, nor kissed her as if her kisses were nectar that he would never get enough of.

With the slick slide of his body covering her, it brought more memories to the forefront of her mind as past and present unfolded like a tight bud blooming to reveal a flower of such outstanding beauty that it couldn't be seen with the human eye.

The movements of Ryu's body within her had her sighing at first with pain then of pleasure. She had felt this mind-numbing desire for Ryu before in their past life, forgetting about it in this one until this moment. Their passion had been banked, smoldering, and never truly forgotten, but ready and waiting to be sparked to life once again.

They never left the bed, yet she felt herself soaring high in the sky, held safely in Ryu's arms as her body responded to his thrusts by clasping her thighs tightly around his hips to hold on as they soared higher. Then, with a rumbling groan, he released them from the coiled tension binding them together to let them fall safely back to reality as they were finally mated and bound, body, mind, and spirit, in this life for all eternity.

"Ryu?" she whispered his name into the glow of the lamp-lighted room while running her hand across his sweat-beaded chest.

He turned his head on the pillow to look at her. "Yes?"

"Itako was right, wasn't she?" Eira said the words her heart knew to be true when she'd first heard them but were only now confirmed. "We're soulmates as well. Our souls have intertwined in this life and in our last."

"No," Ryu said, lightly shaking his head as he held her

loving gaze with his fiercely. "We've been soulmates in *every* life."

Eira hadn't taken the sleeping potion tonight, as she was told it was no longer needed. So, why was her slumber stirred when those strange blue-green eyes entered her dreams?

This nightmare, however, was different, as she took up the girl named Chloe's body. Flashes of her life, like a picture book flipped, appeared before her eyes, and she quickly understood that the wickedly beautiful man named Lucca was actually her lover and was never her enemy at all.

In fact, his method to claim her hadn't been that much different than Ryu staking his claim over Eira at all ...

... She stiffened when he went lower, kissing the scars across her abdomen.

"Beautiful," he murmured as his tongue wiped every memory of Lucifer inflicting them on her. "I'm never going to let anyone hurt you again, baby."

Chloe's breath hitched at the sight and the words he had spoken. How does someone like him exist?

"I know you won't." Her trust in him was unbreakable.

The fire burned hotter than ever when he slid his mouth lower until his bearded lips hovered over her center. "I'm going to have to go to confession," he told her. "God is going to damn me to hell for what I'm about to do."

"W-Wha—"

With the tip of his tongue, he parted her flesh and swiped up and down her slit.

Chloe jumped at the startling sensation, her head falling back and her legs beginning to shake.

He pressed his arm into her thighs, holding her still. Groaning, he then pressed his mouth closer. "A taste of you … is worth a lifetime in hell."

When he increased the pressure of his mouth against her, Chloe felt him sliding his tongue inside of her in quick licks, and then deeper as he became more demanding, more hungered.

Lifting one of her legs over his shoulder, he plunged his tongue into her writhing body.

Oh my God. She began panting. "Take me with you …"

… So, when she woke from her sleep and re-entered this life, she wholly understood.

Those dreams had never been nightmares at all but memories of their past life as Eira and Ryu were once Chloe and Lucca. It had been a good, fulfilling life, with a happy marriage and children, but she knew in her heart that this one was only going to be better.

She also knew instinctively that would be the last time she'd dream of their past, and now she would only ever dream about their wonderful future.

31
UGLY THINGS

When Eira found herself waking alone, it took her a minute to remember that Ryu had told her early in the morning that he had to take care of a few things and that he should be back before she even awoke.

"Guess not," she mumbled, rubbing her eyes. She was simply exhausted and decided she was going to take it easy today. She wished Ryu could do the same, but she figured he still had duties, considering he was to be the future king. All she knew was that they would be crowned in the coming weeks now that they were wed.

Everyone figured it would be best not to overwhelm her with a wedding *and* a coronation. She was grateful for that, and she hoped they'd give her a few days before the topic would be breached.

She went to the bathroom, where she took her time washing up. She was almost done when she heard the doorknob to her bathroom door turn.

"I'll be out in a minute, Ryu," she called out, but instead of Ryu, she was greeted by Yuri's voice.

"Sorry, it's me," her friend quickly announced herself. "I was just checking on you. It's a bit after noon."

"Oh." She found it strange. Usually, Yuri never let herself into her bedroom. She always waited for her outside of the door. Eira guessed she just hadn't heard her knock and grew so concerned that she had let herself in. "I'm fine, just tired."

"I'll wait to help you get dressed for the day."

"That's okay, Yuri; I can get myself dressed. I don't plan on doing much today, anyway."

Yuri could be heard giggling through the door. "I'll let you get your rest before Ryu's return, then."

Eira was glad that she couldn't see her blushing. "Thanks."

"Oh, and Eira," Yuri called out before leaving. "Try using the perfume. I think Ryu would *really* enjoy it."

"I will," she assured her. "See you tomorrow, Yuri."

"Bye," her friend called out, and then Eira was finally alone to finish up.

Looking at the beautiful bottle Yuri had gifted her, she picked it up and was just about to spray herself with it when Yuri's words entered her mind.

"*Try using the perfume.*"

Something about it didn't sit right with her, and then it dawned on her.

How could she know I still haven't used it? For all Yuri knew, she had used it last night when she had come up to her room after the celebration.

Every hair on Eira's body stood on end as her instincts tried to tell her something was amiss, and all she could think about was finding Ryu. She couldn't explain it. Maybe it was because they were mated now, but her instincts told her that she needed protecting, and Ryu's safety.

Quickly, Eira threw on something from the closet and ran to search for him.

Hearing Kage's voice coming from the library, she went to open the cracked door, figuring Ryu was probably with him, when she heard another voice coming from the other side of the door ...

"She still hasn't touched the perfume yet."

If she hadn't talked about the gift, Eira wouldn't even know that the lethal tone had come from Yuri's mouth. Anytime she'd heard her friend speak, butter could melt in her mouth it was so sweet.

"How do you know?" Kage dared to ask.

"Because that *bitch* is still alive," she hissed at her father.

Eira's hand shot up to cover her mouth in shock. Not daring to move in fear they'd find out she was overhearing them, she was forced to continue to listen.

"Your time will come, daughter. She will use the perfume when the time is right. The longer she waits to use it, the less likely anyone will think you laced poison in her gift."

"But if she doesn't die before the coronation, then I'll never be the queen our people will accept. Did you see the way everyone was staring at her last night, in *awe*? It made me *sick* that they'd accept an outsider as their queen!"

"Shh ... Yuri, or someone might hear you." He desperately tried to calm her rising voice, but it was clear Yuri was coming to a breaking point. "I've been reading up on the history of the island again, and while it's rare for a dragon king to take another wife, it has happened before. There's still hope."

"Sorry," Yuri muttered after taking a deep, calming breath. "It's just that if I have to keep pretending to be her friend while she takes all the things I have dreamed of having, I'm going to lose it. I'm running out of ugly things to dress her in, and I already had to watch her wear *my* wedding dress."

"Yes, well, we got unlucky with the poisonous flower, and again when she didn't use the perfume *before* the wedding, but she will. Just give it another day or two, and Ryu, along with all the things we dreamed of, will come true."

"Hmph," Yuri madly pouted. "I wish she would just hurry up, use it, and *die!*"

Oh my—

"I agree." Her father's voice somehow became even more distasteful. "Then those dimwitted grandparents of hers are next."

No!

With that, Eira wasted no time in backing away and running as fast as she could, hoping they didn't hear her take off. Being blindsided by someone she thought was genuinely her friend and Ryu's most trusted people, she could no longer trust *anyone* on this island. There were only two people here who had good intentions for her, and they were now in danger as well.

It wasn't that she thought Ryu didn't care for her. Especially after last night, she knew he did, but how was she supposed to tell him what she had just overheard? She wasn't so sure he'd believe her right away, and Tatsu *definitely* wouldn't. At the end of the day, Ryu had known them much longer than her; she couldn't chance that he might not listen. She could get her grandparents and herself off this godforsaken island, and then Ryu could come find her and decide if she was telling the truth when they were safe.

She fought every instinct in her newly mated, hormone-ridden body not to go to him, but she fought it with all her might, as she must. It was no longer just her life that hung in the balance.

32

THE RED SPIDER LILY
EARLIER THAT MORNING...

Ryu had awoken that morning a bit unsettled. Everything was fine. Great even. However, maybe it was seeing Eira in his mother's wedding dress, but something in his gut felt uneasy about her safety.

Now that she was his wife, Ryu was able to really make changes in his staff and update mandates for her protection, which he planned to do first thing this morning with his father and staff. After the flower incident, he had wanted to enact this immediately, but it was something he could only do *after* they were wed.

He didn't exactly want to spend the morning after his wedding doing this duty, but he was glad he had when he'd woken up with a knot in his stomach.

What he didn't plan on, though, was waking up an hour earlier than planned, but since he couldn't sleep with thoughts of Eira's safety, there was something he could do to pass the time that always helped to bring his mind at ease.

Whispering over to his newly wedded wife that he

would be back before she awoke, he quietly got ready and left the room, heading to his favorite place in the world.

Just going inside the training building made him exhale all the terrible thoughts and release any bad energy he had pent up before he found himself pleasantly surprised to see he wasn't the only one up before dawn.

"Couldn't sleep?"

"You know me," Kage said, not even bothering to open his eyes from his meditation. "But I am surprised that you're up so early. I thought you might be too tired after your big day."

"Yeah ..." was all Ryu could muster to say, not knowing whether to tell him about the uneasy feeling he'd felt the moment he had awoken.

But leave it to his sensei to notice, as one of Kage's eyes peeked open to look at him. "Something bothering you?"

Running his hand through his hair, Ryu remembered Eira asking him the same question he was about to ask. At the time, he had answered so confidently, but now, why was he no longer so a day after their wedding?

"You don't think ... anyone else would try to hurt Eira, do you?"

"The old man is dead, right?" Kage said, getting to his feet with a ready stance. It was obvious his meditation was over. "So, stop your worrying. Eira is perfectly safe here on Kasumi Island."

"Yeah, you're right." Ryu pushed his hair back out of the way, the nervous action revealing it was easier said than done. "I'm just overthinking, is all."

His sensei laughed. "Don't tell me marriage has already made you whipped."

Knowing his longtime friend was only joking, Ryu readied up at his words. "I'll show you whipped."

"Oh"—a bloodthirsty smile touched Kage's lips—"I'd like to see you try."

"Eira, what in the world is wrong?" Her grandmother looked at her as if she were crazy.

"There's no time to explain," she cried, knowing Yuri or Kage could find them at any minute. "We must get a boat and get off the island—now!"

"Oh, honey, I told you I'd get your grandfather to steal a boat *before* you got married, but you're married now." She patted her granddaughter's head not so sympathetically. "Too late."

"I ain't leaving. No way," Grandfather agreed, sipping on an ice-cold drink as if *he* were the king of Kasumi Island. "I've already grown accustomed to a certain way of life."

Eira rolled her eyes, understanding Tatsu a bit more. "Grandfather, we haven't been here that long to get accustomed to anything."

"Well, it's been long enough to know I'm not crossing back over that ocean to drink your grandmother's hot tea again."

When Grandmother went to swat at her husband, Eira knew she needed to knock her own bit of sense into them.

Grabbing her grandmother's arms in a tight vice, she shook her desperately. "Do you trust me?"

Sensing Eira was serious now, she nodded her head. "Yes, of course."

"Then we need to leave," Eira repeated the urgency. "*Now*."

"Honey ..." she called out for her husband's attention.

"Yes, dear?" Grandfather slurped up the last bit of his cold drink through his straw.

"We're leaving."

"Where the hell did she go?" Ryu growled when his father joined him.

"I don't know." His father sounded helpless, catching up to him with even more bad news. "Her grandparents are gone, too."

Red was the only color Ryu saw as he busted down the last room he had yet to check. The library looked like it had been used recently, as a book sat on the table, but it was otherwise empty, causing Ryu to slam his fist down on the desk so hard that it made the book on top fly open.

"Why is no one here? And not a single staff member can locate my wife or tell me her whereabouts before she left the palace?"

"Son, I'm sure they've just gone on a walk ..." Tatsu tried his best to not have Ryu jump to conclusions ... yet.

Thinking only for a moment, Ryu took a calming breath, trying to take his father's advice, but his gut only screamed at him louder. "Something's not right—I can feel it."

Tatsu abruptly nodded. "Then let's ring the gong."

Ryu looked at his father strangely. To ring the gong on the island meant everyone went into life-or-death mode. It was reserved only for the most dire and serious or life-threatening and life-altering consequences.

"You'd do that?"

"Son, I do not wish my fate upon you. You only just

found her; I at least spent many good years with your mother before she passed."

With fists still on the table, Ryu looked down, needing to think for a moment. If they rang the gong and Eira *was* in danger at the hands of someone, it could mean they might only kill her faster. He needed to be strategic and only wished he knew all possibilities before he leaped into action. Deciding he had nothing to go off of, he was just about to tell his father to go through with it when something caught his eye—a hand-drawn flower pasted on the pages of the book.

His anger, or maybe even fate, had conveniently opened it to the all-too-familiar botanical. Flipping the book to look at the cover, he saw the title, *Kasumi Island Family History*.

"What is this?" Ryu asked, mostly to himself, but was shocked to hear his father answer.

"That is Kage's family crest. Tei's are dragons, but Kai's is the red spider lily. You didn't know that?"

Ryu's heart suddenly sank to the floor. "No ..."

"You must not have paid attention to me when I was teaching you the famous family crests, then." Clearing his throat, his father went into the teaching voice he often used when Ryu was a child. "They are said to be very poisonou—"

Tatsu didn't finish his words as both he and Ryu looked at each other with fear in their eyes.

"Oh no." Seeing the writing on the wall for his son, Tatsu felt horrible for him, both of them knowing exactly what must've happened and the betrayal that was happening right under their noses.

Knowing all too well what that look in his son's eyes was, he was almost envious. Tatsu hadn't had anyone to fight when his wife's life had hung in the balance. Fighting an illness was a losing battle against an evil you couldn't take your pain out on. But his son was lucky; lucky that he could fight and possibly save Eira still.

"I'll find Eira; you handle what you need."

"Thanks, Father," was all Ryu said before the dragon under his skin stirred to be let free.

33

IF EIRA'S DEAD, THERE'S NO HOPE FOR YOU

They didn't dare ring the gong, his original fear of it quickening Eira's death if she had been caught a real possibility now. So, he was grateful to find Yuri in the Zen garden, hoping she knew the whereabouts of at least one.

"Have you seen Eira today?" Ryu asked Yuri with urgency.

She sensed his concern, so her sweet tone tried to calm him. "I came to her room earlier, but she said she was tired and sent me away."

Ryu rubbed his temple, still concerned. "And your father?"

"I saw him earlier in the library, but at the moment, I'm not sure." Her concern was evident now. "Is everything all right, Ryu?"

No, it wasn't, but how was he supposed to tell Kage's daughter about her father's betrayal?

"I just need to speak with him—it's urgent." When he turned to leave, Ryu caught a glimpse of something. "What is that?"

"What is—" Yuri stopped when her hand was grabbed by Ryu, who looked upon her fingers up close.

"Why do you have this ring?" he questioned and could sense her surprise that he knew it had been Eira's. There were many things he had collected for his future mate over the course of his life, and he could recall each one. This one in particular was one of his favorite finds. Eira had yet to even wear anything like it, and now he was starting to possibly understand why.

"Oh, um, Eira gifted it for me," she quickly explained with a rising heart rate. "I can't believe you noticed it. She has so many things." She trailed off as her hand began to be squeezed. "Ryu ... you're hurting me."

He didn't even notice that he was squeezing the hand in his like a vice as everything began to click into place.

"What a fool I have been," he whispered harshly. Then, yanking her closer, he could see the slight excitement yet fear that flashed in her eyes.

Using his other hand to hold her chin, the excitement on her features only grew, as it was clear the moment she had been waiting for had finally come ...

But then, suddenly, his hand became as firm as the grip he had on her hand.

"How didn't I see what a jealous, vindictive snake you are before this very moment?"

"I-I ..." The act she tried to continue only lasted a moment longer before she could see in his eyes that there would be no changing his mind—he saw right through her. And with that, the mask began to slip as sweetness faded into her true form. "You have been a fool to fall for an outsider, Ryu."

"Tell me: was it your father who came up with the idea to kill her?"

"Depends," she spat venomously through his grip. "Which time? The flower or the perfume?"

The grip on her face tightened even more as he slipped the ring off her finger with a force that showed he could keep the promise he was about to give. "If Eira's dead, there's no hope for you in this life or the next."

"You wouldn't dare hurt a Kai and a family member of this royal palace!" She hysterically laughed until she trailed off slowly.

And that was when she realized her mistake too late.

"You, Yuri"—Ryu's grip tightened, becoming painful to his victim—"are no family of mine."

Kage was a man of habit, and Ryu knew exactly where to find him. An eerie feeling of déjà vu flashed when Ryu saw Kage doing his meditation exercises, which he continued at Ryu's approach.

Kage merely stared straight ahead, not even bothering to acknowledge his friend's presence.

Oh, how Ryu wished he could go back to earlier this morning before he had known of the gut-wrenching betrayal and stay there, but Ryu wasn't so lucky.

He began to circle his sensei, the teacher whom, until today, he had trusted with his life. Sorrow and fury had his dragon balking at being restrained, wanting to be given full rein on the man who had broken his trust.

"I want to thank you, Kage …"

Kage momentarily paused then resumed his fluid movements as Ryu continued.

"I never could fully understand why the males in my

family had to bear the burden of having our brides chosen for us." Ryu walked around his friend who had turned foe. "And why the fate of our island rested on marrying these women. But if we couldn't find her, we would lose our dragon heritage forever. I don't know if my other male ancestors felt the same way, but I was resentful.

"I admit there were a few of the women in the village I could have settled for, and I resented having the choice made for me. However, thanks to you, I no longer feel that resentment. The prophecy ensured I and my ancestors couldn't be manipulated by others, to prevent evil from entering the dragon line."

Kage made a disgusted sound as he proceeded with his exercise regime. "Your line is weak. The dragon holds so much power, yet never once has it been used to benefit the island. Everyone should be made to fear us, to pay homage to you. Instead, you protect them. Our people still are working as hard as my parents did. We could be rich while our people would never have to work another day."

Ryu folded his hands behind his back as he continued to walk. "How? By using my dragon's existence to inspire fear? The fear wouldn't create wealth; it would lead to the downfall of our people."

"So says our weak prince," his sensei mocked.

"I am not weak. My ancestors were not weak. We are simply not greedy," Ryu spat back, unbelieving of the change in the man who had taught him everything he knew about combat. "How have my father and I not seen you despise us so?"

"Because my ancestors and I did not want you to see. It's not like we could steal the dragon away from your family—it was gifted." Kage put his hands up to the sky to curse whoever that had been. "Unless one of your ancestors had a child with one of mine, then that child could assume the dragon heritage without being stolen. Unfortunately, females aren't often born in our family, and when they were, your ancestors had already mated and birthed the next heir. Yuri is the only female in my lineage who's been born during a time period that could have bred a dragon and heir."

"So, you were prepared to kill anyone I mated with?"

"Yes."

Ryu couldn't believe the brazenness of Kage's admission. "You don't deny it?"

"I said you were weak, not stupid." His backhanded compliment didn't go missed. "Of all the mates you could've had, she was quite easy to want to kill. You should be thankful I have gone to such lengths to rid you of that girl. Eira is a frightened mouse; she doesn't deserve to be queen. The prophecy has been fulfilled. The tree is no longer dying, and nothing has ever been written in history that says only a fated mate can bear a dragon and heir. My daughter will mother excellent children. She will give you a strong warrior, a son to be proud of, not a son afraid of his own shadow. And I guarantee you the tree would restart life again."

"You underestimate Eira. Regardless of whether Eira is in my life or not, I would have never touched Yuri. I feel nothing for her."

"You cannot love Eira. Her beauty does not compare to that of my daughter's." Kage practically laughed. "You would willingly have children with a woman whose relatives have been a source of humiliation since their arrival here?"

"As opposed to having a child with a woman whose father is a murderer?" he mocked.

Unperturbed, Kage didn't even bat an eye. "I have done what is necessary. What *you* should have done yourself."

Ryu stopped dead center in front of Kage. "You are aware I cannot let you go unpunished for your crimes?"

"I am prepared to be banished." He nodded. "It was a price I was willing to pay to have the dragon lineage for my family, which is more than you or your family have done. The dragon was gifted to a line that none of you have done anything to deserve such honor."

Ryu's head fell back in maniacal laughter. "You don't get it, do you, Kage? If you had confined yourself to murdering the villagers, you could have asked them for the mercy of banishment. But you allowed yourself to strike out at Eira—*my mate*—and then attempted to kill her *twice*. She is of the royal house; therefore, the punishment falls onto my shoulders." He let his words sink in for a moment, then continued his taunting, "I am not as merciful as the villagers. There is only one punishment I find acceptable for the crimes you have committed—"

"You think you are capable of killing the man who has trained you since you were a boy?" Amusement filled Kage's expression, which Ryu didn't take personally. Kage made a habit of underestimating others. "You will not be able to best me in your human form. You will have to call forth your dragon. It will be seen from the palace and the training area. How do you think the villagers will react to the dragon killing their beloved sensei? You will only find yourself becoming the outcast."

Ryu's dragon-like gaze didn't waver. "I do not need to call forth my dragon to beat you."

"You cannot beat me in a real battle," Kage scoffed.

Unafraid, Ryu assumed his position. "We shall see."

"We shall." A smiling Kage assumed his own.

Ready to fight to the death, neither bowed to the other, showing their lack of respect for each other.

Readying himself for Kage's attack, the hot-blooded dragon in him demanded him to make the first move. Filling his mind with cold reason, Ryu ignored the dragon's demand. Kage was a master of his art. His family line had trained dragons for centuries; therefore, they were granted the small gift of living a longer life as well, as only when they grew too old to fight were the Teis able to best Kais in combat. Kage had never been beaten, which had only added to his arrogance.

Ryu might be younger, but the master was far from being an old man. His body moved as fluidly as a much younger man's, and he spent hours and hours training students.

Kage came at him, lunging at him like a pouncing tiger, hitting at him like claws aiming for his lungs to drive the oxygen out and to get him to expend his energy on defensive moves. Like a predator, he wanted to weaken his prey before moving in for the killing blow.

However, Ryu blocked the blows, using chi when Kage managed to land a strike. For every strike Kage made, Ryu stomped forward, making strikes of his own.

The two combatants parried blows back and forth. While the two fighting styles allowed Kage to reserve his strength, Ryu had to expend more energy to land harder blows. Kage was banking his defense that he didn't have the stamina to defeat him.

But what Kage didn't take into account was Ryu had started training students, also, and would often become bored in the evenings, deciding to spend them training to become a better instructor. He had actually set himself a goal to become an instructor as good as Kage.

When his sensei had moved the target from his lungs to his arms, pain filled him as one of Kage's moves had him biting back a grunt of pain as the master tried to rip his arm open. Blocking the pain with his chi, Ryu struck at Kage's own arm with a heavy blow at the weakest part.

A distinctive sound of bone snapping had Kage losing momentum for his next strike, his arm hanging uselessly at his side.

Automatically, the master switched his fighting tactics to that of a crane, using his one arm to defend himself and attack. Ryu didn't let Kage switching tactics faze him, sticking to the dragon, sweeping from one side of his opponent to the other. His blows became harder. Fiercer. Determined to beat Kage into the ground for daring to hurt any of the islanders under his protection. Those were the blows he was receiving in punishment. They might hurt a hell of a lot, but they did not kill.

A foot lashed out, aimed at his knee. He was barely able to move in time to let the blow hit the outer side of his thigh.

Limping, Ryu parried with a hard stomp on Kage's foot, grinding the tender flesh under his heel until Kage fell backward. Ryu showed no mercy, driving blow after blow down onto his once trusted friend until the master no longer fought to rise.

"You are a fool, Ryu. A child from you mixed with my blood would have the capacity to become a *legend*." A small trail of blood dribbled from the corner of Kage's mouth.

Ryu stared down at the broken master with pitiless resolve. "A legend you would have tried to make into a monster to be feared and create havoc across the world. Eira brings generations of love with her. Her courage and bravery are shown on her face. You might see Eira as weak, but I see a warrior. A warrior capable of weathering the storms our future holds, compassionate to those who we protect, and most importantly, she will teach our child to hold those same values to keep those like you with evil in their hearts at bay.

"I have served your punishment for the crimes you have committed against the islanders. I will now serve your punishment for attempting to kill Eira." Ryu didn't give Kage time to react, lashing out to rip his windpipe out with a bare hand before throwing it down onto a weakened chest.

Turning away, Ryu gave him his back while Kage choked to death on his own blood.

He came to a halt, seeing his father standing just a few feet away. He had clearly watched it all, as his head hung in sorrow.

"Kage was like a brother to me. His father was my mentor, as Kage was to you. I had no idea of the evil that lurked in his soul."

"Nor did I," Ryu agreed. "Their evil could no longer be hidden once Eira came to the village. He was determined to kill her before we could create a child and the cycle passed on."

At the mention of Eira's name, his father gave a start. "That is why I came here. Her grandfather stole a boat. They are heading back to their home."

"And you didn't stop them?" Ryu asked the obvious, all while he was grateful his mate still walked this plane.

"Son, I think you are forgetting which one of us can still fly."

"Oh, right," Ryu remembered, ready to let his dragon finally be free.

"How do you plan on convincing them to come back?" he asked his son before the transformation was complete.

When Ryu spoke, it was between half-man and half-dragon. "Who's to say I'm going to give them a choice?"

Watching his son proudly start to soar the sky to retrieve his mate, Tatsu had one simple request. "Maybe just convince Eira to come back. You can leave the other two."

34

YOU'VE SEEN RYU EAT SOMEONE?

Eira scanned over the water, hoping to see land coming nearer. Finally, she was able to spot her grandparents' village in the distance.

"We're almost home."

Her grandmother shifted on her ample bottom to look over her shoulder, back to the island they had left. "Can you not make this tub go any faster?"

Her grandfather stopped rowing. "What did you say?"

Eira wanted to scream at her grandfather. "When you're escaping, you don't stop and let them catch up to you!"

"Why are we escaping again? I liked it there."

She could only gape at him. "We're escaping because someone was trying to kill me."

"I'm going to miss being served breakfast in bed." He sighed longingly. "We should go back."

"Old man, I've served you breakfast in bed for the last ten years!"

"You give me porridge. I've gotten used to having a rolled omelet with steamed fish."

"You want fish for breakfast? Then you can get up and go catch it in the morning!" She whacked her husband with each of her words.

Eira wanted to scream at her grandparents for arguing out in the middle of the ocean. "We need to hurry! Here, give me those—"

Her grandfather looked at her like she had lost her mind when she went for the paddles. "What's the hurry? We don't see any boats leaving the island. Even if they left now, they wouldn't be able to reach us before we reached home."

"Give them here, you old fool. I'll do the paddling." Leaving him no choice, she snatched them out of his hands. "You should be ashamed of yourself. You're more concerned about what you're going to have for breakfast instead of your granddaughter's safety."

"I stole the boat, didn't I? You and Eira can stay home. I'll return to the island and keep an eye out for Ryu."

"We don't know if he wanted her dead, too!" her grandmother screeched at him.

She barely managed to keep herself from screeching and sounding just like her. "Grandmother, please ..."

Eira broke off at hearing a swishing sound that had her fearfully raising her gaze.

Ryu, in his dragon form, was hovering above the boat.

Her grandmother, still looking at her, raised her eyes to see what Eira was looking at and started screaming. Her grandfather did the same.

"Ryu, don't—"

A loud *oomph* came out of her when she slid off her seat and onto the floor of the boat as the dragon lifted the boat between his claws and started flying back to the island.

Grabbing her grandmother's skirt, Eira pulled her down

to do the same. Her grandfather quickly did, too, needing no urging, his face ashen.

"Eira, now that we're going to die, I have to admit that we thought you were all crazy when you said Ryu was a dragon." She gulped, still in disbelief that this was happening. "But you meant he was *really* a dragon."

"Obviously!" she screamed loudly at her over the sound of whooshing air.

Grandmother started to practically cry now. "Now he's carrying us off to eat us."

Her husband looked at his plump wife pityingly. "You know he's going to eat you first, don't you?"

"Ryu is not going to eat Grandmother!" she chastised them, but her grandmother only became more hysterical.

"Eira, you cannot have children. My grandchildren can't eat me. My ancestors would never let me rest in peace. They can eat your grandfather when they get hungry."

Eira only buried her face in her curled-up knees, praying that Ryu couldn't hear what they were saying.

"Quit yelling!" her grandfather yelled. "He's going to drop us to shut you up!"

"He's not going to drop his dinner." Her grandmother snorted.

"Ryu is not going to eat either of you," Eira repeated again.

"He doesn't eat humans?"

She sighed not only at the situation she was in, but Eira really hated to lie to her grandmother.

"He does when he's protecting me," she finally admitted.

Now real tears formed in her grandmother's eyes. "You've seen Ryu eat someone?"

There was a time to be truthful, and then there was a

time when it was better to lie like hell. *This is one of those times.*

"No."

"Then how do you know he eats people to protect you?"

"A wild guess," she quipped, just wishing Ryu would drop them to their death at this point.

"You should be surer before making that kind of statement. Your grandfather has a weak heart," her grandmother said, not happy.

"My heart is just fine ... when I'm not flying under a dragon!"

Eira knew she had fucked up the moment Ryu shifted back into his human form the second he had dropped the boat off on the palace's front doorstep.

Her grandmother, concerned about Eira's safety, bravely stepped between them before he could get to her. "Eira's not safe here. Your little friends are evil, so how do we know you aren't, too?"

"Yeah," Grandfather gruffly agreed with a nod when his wife hit his shoulder.

It was a simple and harshly frank answer that the dragon, still raging within from the flight, burst out, "Because I ripped Kage's windpipe out, and then I dropped Yuri off in the middle of the ocean right before I picked you all up in the boat."

All of them stared blankly back at him with their jaws on the ground.

It took her grandmother a few moments to put her still worried thoughts together. "How close did you drop her off next to the shore? She could swim back and want reven—"

"I was flying about a hundred feet high, and if she did survive the fall, she can't swim."

"Welp, that'll do it." Grandfather wiped his hands clean. "I'm going to get some fresh iced tea."

With only her grandmother still standing in his way, she noticed the weak smile she gave her, letting Eira know she was shit out of luck.

"What happens between husband and wife should stay between them."

Watching her grandmother scurry off after her husband, Eira couldn't believe the betrayal. She guessed knowing Ryu wouldn't hurt her was good enough for them, but Eira was still frightened by the way he was furiously staring at her.

"Bedroom—now."

Jumping at his command, she knew better than to defy him as she hurried into the palace and up the steps. Shivers went down her spine the second she entered the confines of her room. She was afraid to turn around and face the dragon, and his next command sent up another chill.

"Eira, look at me."

Slowly turning, she could see the reflection of his dragon in his eyes.

"Why didn't you directly come to me?"

It was a simple question put in a rather harsh tone, yet Eira could hear the hurt in his voice underneath, and along with it was the fear of losing her behind his dragon eyes.

"I'm sorry," she confessed, unable to keep looking into his eyes at the hurt and worry she had caused. "I heard them talking in the library about not only killing me but my grandparents. I know how important Kage and even Yuri were to you, and I was afraid it would take too long to convince you of their plan. Because I wouldn't have believed it myself if *I* hadn't heard it. I knew you would just fly over and meet us at our old home, and you'd find me in a place that was safe, so then I could tell you. I just couldn't risk my grandparents' safety. I'm so sorry, Ryu. I hope you understand."

A part of Ryu's eyes gentled in understanding, but the fire still roared. "Do not ever think I would not believe you over anyone else in this life. Our bond would have told me you were telling the truth, you know."

"Really?" Eira asked, shocked it would have been that easy. "So, you'd know if I ever lied to you?"

Ryu stalked closer now, like a dragon stalking his prey, before he nodded with a devilish smile. "Yes."

"Oh." Eira's stomach fluttered at the way he looked at her as if he wanted to eat her. "That's good to know."

"And one more thing." Ryu tipped her chin up to hold her eyes to his—she always looked away from the dragon roaring inside, but not this time. This time, he was determined she'd face the monster. "If I ever catch you trying to leave this island again without me, I will chain you to this bed forever."

Nodding, she knew it might have sounded like he was only joking, but she knew her fated mate was not.

Only when he was certain she understood did he claim her mouth in a searing kiss that promised he would hold true to his words.

Hoping to be let off easy, she tried to go for the door. "Okay, well, I'm going to go make sure—"

Ryu simply shook his head, startling her to a screeching halt. "I'm not done with you, darling."

Eira cleared her throat, slightly startled for what was to

come. Ryu had promised her that his dragon wouldn't eat her when they made love, but it was hard to believe when it seemed his scales were still fighting to come out from under the surface.

Lazily, Ryu sat down on the edge of the bed, giving her another demand in his husky voice. "Now, undress."

With the way the dragon looked at her now, her clothes practically wanted to fall off her body on their own, so she figured ...

Oh, what the hell.

SEE YOU IN THE NEXT LIFE

Epilogue One

"You wanted to see me?" Tatsu remarked when he entered the room.

Eira had been staring at the beautiful, smoky black vase with golden veins she had been mesmerized by the moment she had first seen it. "Yes." She held on to the cloth-wrapped package that sat in her hands with slight fear. Not wanting to prolong the guilt any longer, she decided to get on with it. "There's something I've been needing to show you."

He looked at her with a raised brow. "Yes?"

Slowly, Eira unwrapped the package to reveal the necklace of his late wife's that had been broken. The shattered look on his face matched the item that only broke her heart in the same amount of pieces. There had been no time to fix it, and without Yuri, she had no one to trust in fixing it now.

"I'm sorry I didn't wear it on our wedding day."

"I wondered why you didn't, but I only thought you didn't think it suited you. But, Eira … what in the world happened to it?"

Her fear grew. She had known he'd be furious. Luckily, she didn't have to lie about her being the one to break it anymore.

"When Yuri took it upstairs to put it away, it broke in her care. She said it was an accident, and even though some things have come to light about her, I'm sure that it was."

"Oh, Eira …" Tatsu carefully took it out of her hands to inspect it closer. "This was no accident."

"It wasn't?" she asked in disbelief, unbelieving Yuri, no matter how truly evil her colors, was capable of doing that to a belonging of Tatsu's late wife's.

But alas …

"No, this was destroyed on purpose and with such hate," he said with disgust.

"So"—Eira bit her lip, not knowing what to think— "you're not mad at me?"

"Of course not," he soothed her fears.

Relieved of any guilt, Eira took a deep breath. "Can you fix it?"

"It might not look the same as it did before, but I should be able to," he said, still inspecting it.

"Oh." Sadness filled her that the piece couldn't be brought back to its former glory. "That's a shame."

Putting the shattered necklace in his pocket, he pointed to the vase Eira had been looking at when he had come in. "Did Ryu ever tell you the story about this vase?"

Eira simply shook her head. "Just that his mother picked it out."

"That she did," he agreed, picking it up himself. He spun the delicate glass in his hands to reveal the gold veins that spanned across all sides. "The day Ryu found out about his mother's illness, he broke it. Much like the necklace, it was no accident and done with powerful emotions. I admit I was quite mad at him for doing it, even though he was young. I expected more—no, too much—out of my son," he corrected himself. "And before my Kana passed from this life, she repaired it."

It was as if Eira could suddenly see the item in a whole new life as Tatsu went on talking and turning the piece in his hands to show off his wife's work proudly.

"It's an old art form called Kintsugi, where you repair what's broken with a precious metal, like gold, and give it new life," he explained where the veins came from. "I remember when she revealed it to Ryu, she told him how something broken could become beautiful again ..."

With a single tear streaking down Eira's face at the touching story, Tatsu gently wiped it away from her just as beautifully scarred face.

"And I couldn't agree more, daughter."

Eira stared out at every islander who slowly began to bow before her. The intricate crown on her head only accentuated the burns on her face that she had grown just as proud to wear, along with the red kimono that was embroidered with gold stitching. It was a flamboyant outfit that made her look as if she was a phoenix rising from the ashes.

And that she was, Ryu thought delightfully of his wife.

Black was no longer a color she clung to, to hide behind, as she wore the Tei family colors with pride now.

Looking out at the love in his people's eyes for their

new queen, the last person he watched bow was a frail old lady who looked as if she were reaching the last of her days.

Itako could only merely bow for a single moment before she smiled at them with such honor. It was obvious she took credit for the match, and watching Eira finally be crowned queen showed her that her duty had been fulfilled.

As he watched the seeress walk away with her cane, Ryu knew it would be the last time he saw her. Itako's voice, carried on the wind, told him that he was right.

See you in the next life.

Epilogue Two

"Another surprise?" Eira asked suspiciously as they headed toward the Sakura tree that they hadn't been under together since they had wed.

"You liked my last surprise," he reminded her.

"One time out of two isn't the best odds."

"True." He laughed, sitting down on the lovely bench, and she sat down next to him. "This one, you will like, too. I think ..."

She gulped nervously, waiting for him to tell her what it was. Growing impatient after several moments, she said, "Well?"

Over the last few days, Eira hadn't felt the best, and maybe it was the anticipation of something good, or bad in this case, that had her feeling as if her lunch might come up at any moment.

"Look up," Ryu said with a kind smile, paying her ill-patience no mind.

Eira did then, looking up at the big, desolate tree with

still only the one cherry blossom sitting upon it at the tippy-top.

"Right"—he tilted her face a bit to see it—"there."

"Is that"—Eira almost couldn't believe it—"a new blossom?"

"Yes." Ryu's smile grew bigger.

"It's starting to regrow." She brightly smiled back. The tree had found new life ...

That was when it began to finally dawn on her.

"Ryu?" Eira gulped rather loudly. "And why is the magical tree starting to regrow *now*?"

Her soul and fated mate's hand touched her belly to hold it in a gentle embrace. "I think you know, darling."

Epilogue Three

The five newly sprouted buds were as if the tree was whispering the promise of a new dragon. Looking over to his father, Ryu swore Tatsu had aged five years overnight.

"Son, there is one last thing I haven't told you about bearing the dragon," he said, his voice sounding just as much older.

Adjusting himself on the bench to sit more comfortably, he didn't understand how there could possibly be something he didn't know. Thinking maybe he was going to tell Ryu that his days of shifting into a dragon were coming to an end, Ryu was prepared to tell him he, of course, already knew that. But that wasn't at all what his father began to say.

"While there is only one dragon that can exist at a time,

there may only be one *former* dragon that can exist at a time as well."

Suddenly, Ryu's heart stopped beating once he understood exactly what his father meant. When his heart began to thump back to life, it was with a vengeance beating madly in his chest. "But that means—"

"I know," Tatsu said, taking his son's hand in a firm yet calming grip.

Heartbroken, Ryu felt the same in this moment as he did when he had found out his mother was destined to die. It had taken him so long to recover. He had finally realized it wasn't until he'd met Eira that he actually fully began to heal from those broken wounds.

With tears streaming down his face, Ryu had to remind himself that a Tei dragon never died and that his ancestors lived on in the heart of his dragon.

Wiping the tears away, he continued on, saying what he was going to, but this time, he wasn't the scared little boy anymore who was losing a parent; he was a man who understood life and death with his own wife and soon-to-be son who depended on him.

"That means"—he cleared his throat—"we only have eight months, if we're lucky."

Tatsu smiled, at peace without any fear of leaving his son, knowing he would see him again in the next plane. "Then let's make them the best eight months to exist."